*Antonio Lopez* ⤙ *Tales from the Thousand*

*and One Nights* ———— *Stewart, Tabori & Chang, Publishers, New York*

*Art coordinator: Juan Ramos*

The publisher gratefully acknowledges the assistance of Alex Gotfryd.

Published by Stewart, Tabori & Chang, Inc.,
740 Broadway, New York, New York 10003

Library of Congress Cataloging in Publication Data

Arabian Nights. English. Selections.
Tales from the Thousand and one nights.

I. Lopez, Antonio.    II. Burton, Richard Francis,
Sir, 1821–1890.    III. Finamore, Roy.    IV. Title.
PJ7716.A1B8    1985    398.2′2    85-7998
ISBN 0-941434-73-7

85 86 87 88 10 9 8 7 6 5 4 3 2 1

Distributed by Workman Publishing
1 West 39 Street, New York, New York 10018

First Edition

Printed in Japan

*Drawings by Antonio Lopez*
*Design by J.C. Suarès*
*Edited by Roy Finamore*
*Adapted from the translation by Sir Richard Burton*

## EDITOR'S FOREWORD

**K**ing Shahryar was unhappy in love. His wife had been unfaithful to him; he had seen other wives unfaithful to their husbands — even a woman unfaithful to an Ifrit who kept her locked in a casket at the bottom of the sea. In an effort to protect his honor, Shahryar resolved to marry only young virgins and to behead them after the bridal night. ⬥ Into this unhappy cavalcade of slaughtered brides comes young Shahrazad who, among other accomplishments, had "collected a thousand books of histories relating to antique races and departed rulers." During her bridal night she begins to tell a tale, "delectable and delightsome," and interrupts it at a crucial moment. Shahryar's interest is piqued; he postpones Shahrazad's execution; she tells her tales for a thousand and one nights; and her husband allows her to live. ⬥ Many years ago Andrew Lang retold several of Shahrazad's stories, but he left out "all the pieces that are suitable only for Arabs and old gentlemen." Sir Richard Burton thought, perhaps, that it was just these pieces that captured Shahryar's attention, and in his translation — long acknowledged as definitive both for its completeness and its aggressive vitality — he seems to omit nothing. Indeed, in his footnotes he expanded on anything at all suitable for "old gentlemen" to make certain the point was not lost. ⬥ Burton took as his task to write "as an Arab would have written in English." In so doing he tended toward the archaic, but he also coined words and altered spellings. The result is a perfect vehicle for Shahrazad's tales. This is not the English we grew up with, and the characters are not people we are likely to meet. But the air of exoticism is fused with a strong sense of familiarity. ➤ Part of the familiarity may come from our having heard at least some of the tales before. We grew up fascinated by stories of jinnis and magic carpets. But we read or were told boiled-down, tidied-up adaptations of adult entertainments. ➤ In this volume we join Shahrazad for thirteen nights of storytelling. She tells of murders, of women changed into gazelles and men into dogs, of betrayal, of evenings of unwedded bliss, of battles between good and evil jinnis. Her stories have not been adapted; they have been edited. The verse, everpresent in Burton's edition, has been removed, and repetitions have been radically pruned — all with the aim of sharpening the focus of the tales. Those events that Andrew Lang might have considered unsuitable for tender minds remain, for they are integral to the stories. ➤ Shahrazad's tales come from another time, another place, and they have long been considered true entertainments. Yes, they are peopled with characters who might be considered fancies of a child's mind, but it is a mistake to consider them children's stories. As a diversion for adults, *The Tales from the Thousand and One Nights* takes many forms. The cast of fiendish demons and beautiful spirits, of good and wicked caliphs and wazirs, of men who understand the language of beasts — all strike a chord. The events, too, seem familiar. Perhaps, deep down, they all represent unexpressed thoughts and desires. Antonio's drawings are familiar in the same way. Perhaps we recognize a face we have once seen, or the way a head is held. It may be that we once caught someone's eye for a moment and in that moment created a history. But these are all suppositions and not of the least importance. What is important is that *The Tales from the Thousand and One Nights* is our opportunity to be diverted, to be charmed, to wander through a garden of bright images.

*R.F.*

IN THE NAME OF ALLAH, THE COMPASSION-ATING, THE COMPASSIONATE! ▪ PRAISE BE TO ALLAH THE BENEFICENT KING ▪ THE CRE-ATOR OF THE UNIVERSE ▪ LORD OF THE THREE WORLDS ▪ WHO SET UP THE FIRMAMENT WITH-OUT PILLARS IN ITS STEAD AND WHO STRETCHED OUT THE EARTH EVEN AS A BED AND GRACE ▪ AND PRAYER-BLESSING BE UPON OUR LORD MOHAM-MED ▪ LORD OF APOSTOLIC MEN ▪ AND UPON HIS FAMILY AND COMPANION-TRAIN ▪ PRAYER AND BLESSINGS ENDURING AND GRACE WHICH UNTO THE DAY OF DOOM SHALL REMAIN ▪ AMEN! ▪ O THOU OF THE THREE WORLDS SOVEREIGN!

## THE TALE OF KING SHAHRYAR AND HIS BROTHER

In tide of yore and in time long gone before, there was a King of the Banu Sasan in the Islands of India and China, a Lord of armies and guards and servants and dependents. He left only two sons, one in the prime of manhood and the other yet a youth. So the elder succeeded to the empire, and lorded it over his lieges with justice so exemplary that he was beloved by all the peoples of his kingdom. His name was King Shahryar, and he made his younger brother, Shah Zaman, King of Samarcand in Barbarian-land. Each ruled his own kingdom, and this condition continually endured for a score of years. ———But at the end of the twentieth twelvemonth the elder King yearned for a sight of his younger brother and felt that he must look upon him once more. So he took counsel with his Wazir about visiting him. But the Minister recommended that a letter be written and a present be sent to the younger brother with an invitation to visit the elder. ———Having accepted this advice the King forthwith prepared handsome gifts, such as horses with saddles of gem-encrusted gold; Mamelukes, or white slaves; beautiful handmaids, high-breasted virgins, and splendid stuffs and costly. He then wrote a letter to Shah Zaman expressing his warm love and great wish to see him, ending with these words, "Our one and only desire is to see thee ere we die; but if thou delay or disappoint us we shall not survive the blow." ———Then King Shahryar, having sealed the missive, gave it to the Wazir and commanded him to shorten his skirts and strain his strength and make all expedition in going and returning. ———"Harkening and obedience!" quoth the Minister, who took leave of his King and marched right away, over desert and hillway, stony waste and pleasant lea without halting by night or by day. ———As soon as the Wazir entered Samarcand he proceeded straightway to the palace, where he presented himself in the

royal presence; and, after kissing ground and praying for Shah Zaman's health and happiness and for victory over all his enemies, he delivered the letter, which Shah Zaman took from his hand and said, "I hear and I obey the commands of the beloved brother!" Then he caused his tents and camels and mules to be brought forth and encamped, with their bales and loads, attendants and guards, within sight of the city, in readiness to set out next morning for his brother's capital. ━━━When the night was half spent he bethought him that he had forgotten in his palace somewhat which he should have brought with him, so he returned and entered his apartments. There he found the Queen, his wife, asleep on his own carpet-bed, embracing with both arms a black cook of loathsome aspect and foul with kitchen grease and grime. When he saw this the world waxed black before his sight and he said, "If such case happen while I am yet within sight of the city what will be the doings of this damned whore during my long absence at my brother's court?" So he drew his scymitar and, cutting the two in four pieces with a single blow, left them on the carpet and returned to his camp. Then he gave orders for immediate departure; but he could not help thinking over his wife's treason and he kept ever saying to himself, "How could she do this deed by me? How could she work her own death?" till excessive grief seized him and his body waxed weak. ━━━When the brothers met, the elder could not but see the change of complexion in the younger, and he questioned him. ━━━"O my brother, I see thou art grown weaker of body and yellower of colour." ━━━Shah Zaman replied, "I have an internal wound." But he would not tell him what he had witnessed in his wife. ━━━Shahryar summoned doctors and surgeons and bade them treat his brother according to the rules of art, which they did for a whole month; but their sherbets and potions naught availed, and despondency, instead of diminishing, prevailed. ━━━One day his elder brother said to him, "I am going forth to hunt and to take my pleasure and pastime; maybe this would lighten thy heart." Shah Zaman, however, refused; and next morning,

when his brother had fared forth, Shah Zaman sat down at one of the lattice-windows overlooking the pleasure-grounds. There he abode thinking with saddest thought over his wife's betrayal, and burning sighs issued from his tortured breast. And as he continued in this case lo! a postern of the palace, which was carefully kept private, swung open and out of it came twenty slave girls surrounding his brother's wife, who was a model of beauty and comeliness and symmetry and loveliness. They walked into the garden till they came to a jetting fountain amid a great basin of water; then they stripped off their clothes and behold, ten of them were women, concubines of the King, and the other ten men. They all paired off, each with each: but the Queen, who was left alone, cried out in a loud voice, "Here to me, O my lord Saeed!" and then sprang with a drop-leap from one of the trees a big slobbering blackamoor. He walked boldly up to her and threw his arms round her neck; then he bussed her and, winding his legs round hers, as a button-loop clasps a button, he enjoyed her. Now, when Shah Zaman saw this conduct of his sister-in-law he said in himself, "By Allah, my calamity is lighter than this! My brother is a greater King among the kings than I am, yet this infamy goeth on in his very palace, and his wife is in love with that filthiest of filthy slaves. But this only showeth that they all do it, and that there is no woman but who cuckoldeth her husband." So he put away his melancholy and despondency, regret and repine, and allayed his sorrow by constantly repeating those words, adding, " 'Tis my conviction that no man in this world is safe from their malice!" His brother came back from the chase ten days after, and when King Shahryar looked at King Shah Zaman he saw how the hue of health had returned to him. He wondered much and said, "I beseech thee to explain the reason of thy recovery. So speak out and hide naught!" Thereupon Shah Zaman told him all he had seen, from commencement to conclusion, ending with these words, "When I beheld thy calamity and the treason of thy wife, O my brother, mine own sorrow was belittled by the comparison, and my mind recovered tone and temper." ～～ When King Shahryar heard this, rage was like to strangle him; but he said, "O my brother, I cannot credit it till I see it with mine own eyes." Whereupon he let make proclamation of his intent to travel, and the troops and tents fared forth. ～～ Then the brothers disguised themselves and returned by night with all secrecy to the palace, and they seated themselves at the lattice overlooking the pleasure grounds. The Queen and her handmaids came out as before, and made for the fountain. Here they stripped, and the King's wife called out, "Where art thou, O Saeed?" The hideous blackamoor dropped from the tree straightway; and, rushing into her arms without stay or delay, cried out, "I am Sa'ad al-Din Saood!" The lady laughed heartily, and all fell to satisfying their lusts. ～～When King Shahryar saw this infamy of his wife he became as one distraught and he cried out, "Only in utter solitude can man be safe from the doings of this vile world! Let us up as we are and depart forthright hence, for we have no concern with Kingship, and let us overwander Allah's earth, worshipping the Almighty till we find some one to whom the like calamity hath happened; and if we find none then will death be more welcome to us than life." ～～ So the two brothers betook themselves from the palace, and they never stinted wayfaring by day and by night, until they reached a tree a-middle of a meadow hard by a spring of sweet water on the shore of the salt sea. Both drank of it and sat down to take their rest; and lo! they heard a mighty roar, and the sea brake with waves before them, and from it towered a black pillar, which grew and grew till it rose skywards and began making for that meadow. Seeing it, they waxed fearful exceedingly and climbed to the top of the tree, which was lofty; whence they gazed to see what might be the matter. ～～ It was a Jinni, an Ifrit huge of height and burly of breast and bulk, bearing on his head a coffer of crystal. He strode to land, wading through the deep, and coming to the tree, seated himself beneath it. He then set down the coffer, drew out a casket, with seven padlocks of steel, which he unlocked with seven keys of steel. Out of the casket came a

young woman, white-skinned and of winsome mien, of stature fine and thin, and bright as the sun raining lively sheen. The Jinni seated her under the tree by his side, and he then laid his head upon the lady's thighs; and, stretching out his legs, he slept. Presently the winsome woman raised her head towards the treetop and saw the two Kings. "Come ye down, ye two, and fear naught from this Ifrit." They were in a terrible fright and answered, "Allah upon thee and by thy modesty, O lady, excuse us from coming down!" But she rejoined, "If ye come not, I will rouse upon you my husband, this Ifrit, and you shall die by the illest of deaths." So, being afraid, they came down to her and she rose before them and said, "Stroke me a strong stroke, without stay or delay." They said to her, "O our lady, how then can we do as thou desirest?" "Leave this talk," quoth she, and she swore that, if they worked not her will, she would cause them to be slain and cast into the sea. Whereupon, by reason of their sore dread of the Jinni, both did by her what she bade them do; and, when they had dismounted from her, she said, "Well done!" She then took from her pocket a purse and drew out a knotted string, whereon were strung five hundred and seventy seal rings, and she asked, "Know ye what be these?" They answered her saying, "We know not!" "These be the signets of five hundred and seventy men who have all futtered me upon the horns of this foul, this foolish, this filthy Ifrit; so give me also your two seal rings, ye pair of brothers." When they had drawn their two rings from their hands and given them to her, she said to them, "Of a truth this Ifrit bore me off on my bride-night, and put me into a casket and set the casket in a coffer and to the coffer he affixed seven strong padlocks of steel and deposited me on the deep bottom of the sea that raves, dashing and clashing with waves, and guarded me so that I might remain chaste and honest, that none save himself might have connexion with me. But I have lain under as many of my kind as I please. Now wend your ways and bear yourselves beyond the bounds of his malice." So they fared forth saying either to other "Allah! Allah!" and, "There be no Majesty and there be no Might save in Allah, the Glorious, the Great; and with Him we seek refuge from women's malice and sleight. Consider, O my brother, the ways of this marvellous lady with an Ifrit who is so much more powerful than we are. Now since there hath happened to him a greater mishap than that which befel us and which should bear us abundant consolation, so return we to our countries and capitals, and we will show them what will be our action." Thereupon they returned to the city, and there King Shahryar sat him upon his throne and, sending for the Wazir, he said, "I command thee to take my wife and smite her to death; for she hath broken her plight and her faith." Then King Shahryar took brand in hand and slew all the concubines. He then sware himself by a binding oath that whatever wife he married he would abate her maidenhead at night and slay her next morning to make sure of his honour; "For," said he, "there never was nor is there one chaste woman upon face of earth." Shahryar commanded his Wazir to bring him a bride; so he produced a most beautiful girl, the daughter of one of the Emirs, and the King went in unto her at eventide and when morning dawned he bade his Minister strike off her head. And the Wazir did. On this wise he continued for the space of three years; marrying a maiden every night and killing her the next morning. And women made an uproar and mothers wept and parents fled with their daughters. And the Minister went forth and searched for a virgin and found none. Now the Wazir had two daughters, Shahrazad and Dunyazad. Of the elder it was said that she had collected a thousand books of histories relating to antique races and departed rulers. She had perused the works of the poets and knew them by heart; she had studied philosophy and the sciences, arts and accomplishments; and she was pleasant and polite, wise and witty, well read and well bred. Now on that day she said to her father, "Why do I see thee thus changed and laden with care?" The Wazir related to her, from first to last, all that had happened between him and the King.

Thereupon said she, "By Allah, O my father, how long shall this slaughter of women endure? Shall I tell thee what is in my mind in order to save both sides from destruction?" ——— "Say on, O my daughter," quoth he. ——— "I wish thou wouldst give me in marriage to this King Shahryar; either I shall live or I shall be a ransom for the virgin daughters of Moslems and the cause of their deliverance from his hands and thine." ——— The Wazir was moved to fury and blamed and reproached her, ending with, "In very deed I fear lest the same befal thee which befel the Bull and the Ass with the Husbandman." ——— Whereupon the Wazir began

## THE TALE OF THE BULL AND THE ASS

Know, O my daughter, that there was once a merchant who owned much money and who was rich in cattle and camels; he had also a wife and family and he dwelt in the country. Now Allah Most High had endowed him with understanding the tongues of beasts and birds of every kind, but promised pain of death if he divulged the gift to any. So he kept it secret for very fear. He had in his cow-house a Bull and an Ass each tethered in his own stall one hard by the other. One day he heard the Bull say to the Ass, "Hail and health to thee O Father of Waking! for that thou enjoyest rest and good ministering, while I (unhappy creature!) am led forth in the middle of the night, when they set on my neck the plough and a something called Yoke; and I tire at cleaving the earth from dawn of day till set of sun. They take me back with my sides torn, my neck flayed, my legs aching and mine eyelids sored with tears. Then they shut me up in the byre and throw me beans and crushed straw, mixed with dirt and chaff; and I lie in dung and filth and foul stinks through the livelong night. But thou art ever in a place swept and sprinkled and cleansed, and thou art always lying at ease, save when the master has some small business. So it happens that I am toiling and distrest while thou takest thine ease and thy rest; thou sleepest while I am sleepless; I hunger still while thou eatest thy fill, and I win contempt while thou winnest good will." When the Bull ceased speaking, the Ass said, "O thou lost one! he lied not who dubbed thee Bull-head, for thou art the simplest of simpletons. Now hearken to me, Sir Bull! If thou accept my advice it will be better for thee and thou wilt lead an easier life even than mine. When thou goest a-field and they lay the yoke on thy neck, lie down and rise not

again; and when they bring thee home and offer thee thy beans, fall backwards and taste it not. Feign thou art sick, and cease not doing thus for a day or two days or even three days, so shalt thou have rest from toil and moil." ⸺When the Bull heard these words he knew the Ass to be his friend and thanked him. ⸺(Now the merchant, O my daughter, understood all that passed between them.) ⸺Next day the driver took the Bull, but the Bull began to shirk his ploughing, according to the advice of the Ass, and the ploughman drubbed him till he broke the yoke. Not the less, however, would he do nothing but stand still and drop down till the evening. Then the herd led him home and stabled him in his stall: but he drew back from his manger and neither stamped nor ramped nor butted nor bellowed as he was wont to do; whereat the man wondered. He brought him the beans and husks, but the Bull left them and lay down as far from them as he could and passed the whole night fasting. ⸺The peasant came next morning; and, seeing the manger full of beans, the crushed straw untasted and the ox lying on his back with legs outstretched and swollen belly, he was concerned for him. Then he went to the merchant and reported, "O my master, the Bull is ailing; he refused his fodder last night; nay more, he hath not tasted a scrap of it this morning." The merchant-farmer quoth, "Take that rascal donkey, and set the yoke on his neck, and bind him to the plough and make him do Bull's work." ⸺The ploughman took the Ass, and worked him through the livelong day at the Bull's task; and, when the Ass failed for weakness, the ploughman made him eat stick till his ribs were sore and his sides were sunken and his neck was flayed by the yoke; and when he came home in the evening he could hardly drag his limbs along. But the Bull had passed the day lying at full length, and had eaten his fodder with an excellent appetite, and he ceased not calling down blessings on the Ass for his good advice. So when night set in and the Ass returned to the byre the Bull rose up before him in honour, and said, "May good tidings gladden thy heart, O Father Wakener! through thee I have rested all this day and I have eaten my meat in peace and quiet." But the Ass returned no reply, for wrath and heart-burning and fatigue and the beating he had gotten; and he repented with the most grievous of repentance; and quoth he to himself: "This cometh of my folly in giving good counsel. And now I must take thought and put a trick upon him and return him to his place, else I die."———"And even so, O my daughter," said the Wazir, "thou wilt die for lack of wits; therefore sit thee still and say naught and expose not thy life to such stress."———"O my father," Shahrazad answered, "I must go up to this King and be married to him."———"If thou be not silent and bide still," he rejoined, "I will do with thee even what the merchant did with his wife."———"And what did he?"———After the return of the Ass the merchant came out on the terrace-roof with his wife and family, for it was a moonlit night and the moon at its full. Now the terrace overlooked the cow-house and presently the trader heard the Ass say to the Bull, "Tell me, O Father Broad o'Brow, what thou purposest to do to-morrow?" The Bull answered, "What but continue to follow thy counsel? Indeed it was as good as good, and it hath given me rest and repose; nor will I now depart from it one tittle."———The Ass shook his head and said, "Beware of so doing, O Father of a Bull!"———The Bull asked, "Why?" and the Ass answered, "Know that I am about to give thee the best of counsel, for verily I heard our owner say to the herd, 'If the Bull rise not from his place to do his work this morning, and if he retire from his fodder this day, make him over to the butcher that he may slaughter him.' So take my advice ere a calamity befal thee; and when they bring thee thy fodder eat it and rise up and bellow and paw the ground, or our master will assuredly slay thee!" Thereupon the Bull arose and lowed aloud and thanked the Ass; and he at once ate up all his meat and even licked the manger.———(All this, my daughter, took place while the owner was listening to their talk.)———Next morning the trader and his wife went to the Bull's crib and sat down, and the driver came and led forth the Bull who, seeing his owner, whisked his tail and brake wind, and frisked about so lustily that the merchant laughed a loud laugh and kept laughing till he fell on his back. His wife looked on and asked him, "Whereat laughest thou with such loud laughter as this?"⟶ And he answered her, "I laughed at a secret something which I have heard and seen but cannot say lest I die my death."⟶ She returned, "By Allah, thou liest! thou laughest at none save me, and now thou wouldst hide somewhat from me. But by the Lord of the Heavens! if thou disclose not the cause I will leave thee." And she sat down and cried; and she ceased not to importune him till he was worn out and clean distraught. ⟶ So at last he determined to reveal to her his secret and die the death; for he loved her with love exceeding because she was his cousin, the daughter of his father's brother, and the mother of his children, and he had lived with her a life of a hundred and twenty years. ⟶ Now that merchant had in his out-houses some fifty hens under one cock, and whilst making ready to farewell his folk he heard one of his many farm-dogs thus address in his own tongue the Cock, who was flapping his wings and crowing lustily and jumping from one hen's back to another and treading all in turn, saying "O Chanticleer! how mean is thy wit and how shameless is thy conduct! Art thou not ashamed of thy doings on such a day as this?"⟶ "And what," asked the Rooster, "hath occurred this day?"⟶ "Dost thou not know that our master is this day making ready for his death? His wife is resolved that he shall disclose the secret taught to him by Allah, and the moment he so doeth he shall surely die."⟶ "Then," quoth the Cock, "is our master a lack-wit and a man scanty of sense: if he cannot manage matters with a single wife, his life is not worth prolonging. Now I have some fifty Dame Partlets; and I please this and provoke that and starve one and stuff another; and through my good governance they are all well under my control. This our master pretendeth to wit and wisdom, and he hath but one wife; yet knoweth not how to manage her."⟶ Asked the Dog, "What then, O Cock, should the master do to win clear of his strait?"⟶ "He should arise

forthright," answered the Cock, "and take some twigs from yon mulberry-tree and give her a regular back-basting and rib-roasting till she cry: 'I repent, O my Lord! I will never ask thee a question as long as I live!' Then let him beat her once more, and soundly, and when he shall have done this he shall sleep free from care and enjoy life." ━━➤ When the merchant heard the wise words spoken by his Cock to his Dog, he arose in haste and, after cutting some mulberry-twigs and hiding them, he called to his wife, "Come that I may tell thee the secret; and while no one seeth me, die." ━━➤ She entered with him and he locked the door and came down upon her with so sound a beating of back and shoulders, arms and legs, saying the while, "Wilt thou ever be asking questions about what concerneth thee not?" She cried out, "By Allah, I will ask thee no more questions, and indeed I repent sincerely and wholesomely." Then she kissed his hand and feet and he led her out of the room submissive as a wife should be. ━━➤ Thus the merchant learnt family discipline from his Cock and he and his wife lived together the happiest of lives. ━━➤ "And thou also, O my daughter!" continued the Wazir, "Unless thou turn from this matter I will do by thee what that trader did to his wife." ━━➤ But Shahrazad answered him with much decision. "Leave such talk and tattle. If thou deny me, I will marry myself to him despite the nose of thee." ━━➤ Hereupon the Wazir, being weary of lamenting and contending, persuading and dissuading her, all to no purpose, went

up to King Shahryar and told him all about his daughter from first to last and how he designed to bring her to him that night. The King wondered with exceeding wonder; for he had made an especial exception of the Wazir's daughter, and said to him, "O most faithful of Counsellors, how is this? Thou knowest that I have sworn by the Raiser of the Heavens that after I have gone in to her this night I shall say to thee on the morrow's morning: 'Take her and slay her!' and, if thou slay her not, I will slay thee in her stead without fail." ⬩⬩⬩ "O King of the age," answered the Wazir, "she will not hearken to me and she persisteth in passing this coming night with the King's Majesty." So Shahryar said, " 'Tis well; go get her ready and this night bring her to me." ⬩⬩⬩ Shahrazad rejoiced with exceeding joy and said to her younger sister, Dunyazad, "Note well what directions I entrust to thee! When I have gone in to the King I will send for thee and when thou comest to me and seest that he hath had his carnal will of me, do thou say to me: 'O my sister, relate to me some new story, delectable and delightsome, the better to speed our waking hours,' and I will tell thee a tale which shall be our deliverance." ⬩⬩⬩ So when it was night their father the Wazir carried Shahrazad to the King. But when the King took her to his bed and fell to toying with her she wept; which made him ask, "What aileth thee?" ⬩⬩⬩ She replied, "O King of the age, I have a younger sister and lief would I take leave of her this night." ⬩⬩⬩ So he went at once for Dunyazad and she came and he permitted her to take her seat near the foot of the couch. Then the King arose and did away with his bride's maidenhead. And Shahrazad signalled to Dunyazad who said, "O my sister, recite to us some new story, delightsome and delectable." ⬩⬩⬩ "With joy and goodly gree," answered Shahrazad, "if this pious and auspicious King permit me." ⬩⬩⬩ "Tell on," quoth the King, who chanced to be sleepless and restless and therefore was pleased with the prospect of hearing a story. ⬩⬩⬩ So Shahrazad rejoiced; and thus, on the first night of the Thousand Nights and a Night, she began with

# THE TALE OF THE TRADER AND THE JINNI

It is related, O auspicious King, that there was a merchant of the merchants who had much wealth. Now one day he mounted horse and went forth to recover monies in certain towns, and the heat sore oppressed him; so he sat beneath a tree and took some dry dates. When he had ended eating the dates he threw away the stones with force and lo! an Ifrit appeared, huge of stature and brandishing a drawn sword, wherewith he approached the merchant and said, "Stand up that I may slay thee, even as thou slewest my son!" ⟋ Asked the merchant, "How have I slain thy son?" ⟋ "When thou threwest away the stones they struck my son, so that he died forthwith." ⟋ Quoth the merchant, "If I slew thy son, I slew him by chance. I pray thee pardon me." ⟋ "There is no help but I must slay thee." Then the Jinni seized him and, casting him to the earth, raised the sword to strike him; whereupon the merchant wept, and said, "O thou Ifrit, I have children and a wife; so permit me to go home and I will come back to thee at the head of the new year. Allah be my testimony and surety that I will return to thee; and then thou mayest do with me as thou wilt." ⟋ The Jinni took sure promise of him and let him go; so he returned to his own city and after informing his wife and children of what he betided him, took his shroud under his arm and bade farewell to his people, his neighbours and all his kith and kin, and went forth despite his own nose. They then began weeping and wailing and beating their breasts over him; but he travelled until he arrived at the same garden. ⟋ As he sat weeping over what had befallen him, behold! a Shaykh, a very ancient man, drew near leading a chained gazelle; and he saluted the merchant and said, "What is the cause of thy sitting in this resort of evil spirits?" The merchant related to him what had come to pass, and the old man wondered and said, "By Allah, O brother, thy story is right strange. I will not leave thee until I see what may come to pass with thee and this Ifrit." ⟶ And presently a second Shaykh approached them, and with him were two dogs both of greyhound breed and both black. The second old man, after saluting them with the salam, also asked "What causeth you to sit in this place?" So they told him the tale from beginning to end, and their stay there had not lasted long before there came up a third Shaykh, and with him a she-mule of bright bay coat; and he saluted them and asked them why they were seated in that place. So they told him the story from first to last. ⟶ And lo! a dust-cloud advanced and the cloud opened and behold! within it was that Jinni holding in hand a drawn sword, while his eyes were shooting fire-sparks of rage. He came up to them and cried to the merchant, "Arise that I may slay thee, as thou slewest my son!" The merchant wailed and wept, and the three old men began sighing and crying and weeping and wailing. Presently the first old man kissed the hand of the Ifrit and said, "O Jinni, thou Crown of the Kings of the Jann! were I to tell the story of me and this gazelle and thou shouldst consider it wondrous, wouldst thou give me a third part of this merchant's blood?" ⟶ Quoth the Jinni, "O Shaykh! if thou tell me this tale, and I hold it a marvellous, then will I give thee a third of his blood." Thereupon the old man began to tell

41

Now, O Jinni! that this gazelle is the daughter of my paternal uncle, my own flesh and blood, and I married her when she was a young maid, and I lived with her well-nigh thirty years, yet was I not blessed with issue by her. So I took me a concubine, who brought to me a male child fair as the full moon. Little by little he grew in stature, and when he was a lad fifteen years old, it became needful I should journey to certain cities and I travelled. But the daughter of my uncle (this gazelle) bewitched that son of mine to a calf and my handmaid (his mother) to a heifer, and made them over to the herdsman's care. ———— Now when I returned and asked for my son and his mother, she answered me, saying "Thy slave-girl is dead, and thy son hath fled." So I remained for a whole year with grieving heart and streaming eyes until the time came for the Great Festival of Allah. Then sent I to my herdsman bidding him choose for me a fat heifer; and he brought me my handmaid, whom this gazelle had ensorcelled. She lowed aloud and wept bitter tears. I marvelled, but I commanded the herdsman to slay her. He killed her and skinned her but found in her neither fat nor flesh, only hide and bone. ———— I then said to the herdsman, "Fetch me a fat calf," and he brought my son ensorcelled. ———— When the calf saw me, he ran to me and fawned upon me and wailed and shed tears so that I took pity on him and said to the herdsman, "Bring me a heifer and let this calf go!" Thereupon my cousin (this gazelle) called aloud, "Thou must kill this calf. This is a holy day and a blessed, whereon naught is slain save what be perfect-pure; and we have not amongst our calves any fatter or fairer than this! And if thou kill him not to me thou art no man and I to thee am no wife." ———— Now when I heard those hard words, not knowing her object I went up to the calf, knife in hand — — And Shahrazad perceived the dawn of day and ceased to say her say. Then quoth her sister to her, "How fair is thy tale, and how grateful, and how sweet and how tasteful!" Shahrazad answered, "What is this to that I could tell, were the King to spare me?" Then said the King, "By Allah, I will not slay her, until I shall have heard the rest of her tale."

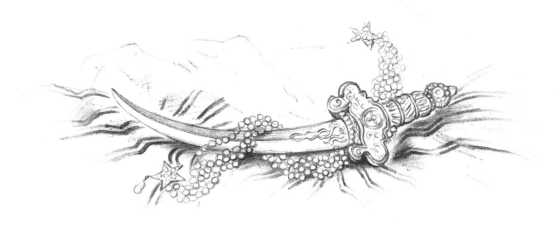

*When it was the Second Night*

Dunyazad said to Shahrazad, "O my sister, finish for us that story of the Merchant and the Jinni." And she answered, "With joy and goodly gree, if the King permit me." Then quoth the King, "Tell thy tale," and Shahrazad began. It hath reached me, O auspicious King and Heaven-directed Ruler! that when the merchant purposed the sacrifice of the calf but saw it weeping, his heart relented. All this the old Shaykh told the Jinni who marvelled much at these strange words. Then the owner of the gazelle continued. O Lord of the Kings of the Jann, this much took place and my uncle's daughter, this gazelle, looked on and saw it, and said, "Butcher me this calf, for surely it is a fat one," but I bade the herdsman take it away. On the next day as I was sitting in my own house, lo! the herdsman came and said, "O my master, I will tell thee a thing which shall gladden thy soul. I have a daughter, and she learned

43

magic in her childhood from an old woman. Yesterday when thou gavest me the calf, I went into the house to her, and she looked upon it and veiled her face; and at last she said, 'O my father, hath mine honour become so cheap to thee that thou bringest in to me strange men?' I asked her: 'Where be these strange men?' and she answered, 'Of a truth this calf is the son of our master, but his stepdame bewitched both him and his mother.'" When I heard, O Jinni, my herdsman's words, I was drunken without wine, from the excess of joy and gladness which came upon me. I rejoiced, and went to the herdsman's daughter, and said, "O maiden, if thou wilt release him thine shall be whatever property of mine are under thy father's hand." She smiled and answered, "O my master, I have no greed for the goods nor will I take them save on two conditions: first, thou must marry me to thy son and second, I must bewitch her who bewitched him." Now when I heard, O Jinni, these words, I replied, "Beside what thou askest all the cattle and the household stuff in thy father's charge are thine." When I had spoken she took a cup and filled it with water. Then she recited a spell over it and sprinkled it upon the calf, saying, "If Almighty Allah created thee a calf, remain so shaped, and change not; but if thou be enchanted, return to thy whilom form, by command of Allah Most Highest!" and lo! he trembled and became a man. Then, O Jinni, I married the herdsman's daughter to him, and she transformed my wife into this gazelle. I took this gazelle (my cousin) and wandered with her from town to town, till Destiny drove me to this place where I saw the merchant sitting in tears. Such is my tale! Quoth the Jinni, "This story is indeed strange, and therefore I grant thee the third part of his blood." Thereupon the second old man, who owned the two greyhounds, came up and said, "O Jinni, if I recount to thee what befel me, and thou see that it is a tale even more wondrous and marvellous than what thou hast heard, wilt thou grant to me also the third of this man's blood?" Replied the Jinni, "Thou hast my word for it." Thereupon he thus began

THE SECOND SHAYKH'S STORY

Know, O lord of the Kings of the Jann! that these two dogs are my brothers and I am the third. Now when our father died and left us a capital of three thousand gold pieces, I opened a shop, and in like guise did my two brothers; but the elder soon sold his stock and went his ways to foreign parts. One day as I sat in my shop, behold! a beggar stood before me asking alms and weeping, "Am I so changed that thou knowest me not?" and lo! it was my brother. ◆ I found that industry had gained me wealth, so I shared the whole with him saying, "Be not cast down by thine ill-luck." He took the share in great glee and opened for himself a shop; and matters went on quietly for a few nights and days. ◆ But presently my second brother (yon other dog) also set his heart upon travel. After an absence of a whole year he came back to me and cried, "O my brother, here I am a mere beggar, penniless and without a shirt to my back." So, O Jinni, clothing him in new clothes, I made over one half of my profit to my brother, keeping the other to myself. Thereupon he busied himself with opening a shop and on this wise we abode many days. ◆ After a time my brothers began pressing me to travel with them; but I refused to do so till full six years were past and gone when I consented. ◆ We then got ready suitable goods and hired a ship and proceeded on our voyage. We arrived at a city where we sold our goods, and for every piece of gold we gained ten. And as we turned again to our voyage we found on the shore of the sea a maiden clad in worn and ragged gear, and she kissed my hand and said, "Take me to wife, O my master, and carry me to thy city, for I have given myself to thee; so do me a kindness and I will make thee a fitting return." So we

voyaged on, and my heart became attached to her with exceeding attachment, and I was separated from her neither night nor day. My brothers waxed jealous, and their eyes were opened covetously upon all my property. So they took counsel to murder me and seize my wealth. So when they found me in privacy (and I sleeping by my wife's side) they took us both up and cast us into the sea. My wife awoke startled from her sleep and, forthright becoming an Ifritah, she bore me up and carried me to an island, and said, "Here am I, thy faithful slave, who hath made thee due recompense; for I saved thee from death. Know that I am a Jinniyah, and as I saw thee my heart loved thee by will of the Lord, for I am a believer in Allah and in His Apostle (whom Heaven bless and preserve!). But I am angered against thy brothers and assuredly I must slay them."

When I heard her story I was surprised and, thanking her for all she had done, I said, "But as to slaying my brothers this must not be." I humbled myself before her for their pardon, whereupon she bore me up and flew away with me till at last she set me down on the terrace-roof of my own house. Now when night came, I saw these two hounds tied up; but ere I knew what happened my wife said, "These two dogs be thy brothers!" I answered, "And who hath done this thing by them?" She rejoined, "I sent a message to my sister and she entreated them on this wise, nor shall these two be released from their present shape till ten years shall have passed." And now I have arrived at this place on my way to my wife's sister that she may deliver them from this condition. Such is my tale! Said the Jinni, "Surely this is a strange story and therefore I give thee the third portion of his blood."

Thereupon quoth the third Shaykh to the Jinni, "I can tell thee a tale more wondrous than these two, so thou grant me the remainder of his blood," and the Jinni answered, "So be it!" Then the old man began

THE THIRD SHAYKH'S STORY

Know, O Sultan and head of the Jann, that this mule was my wife. Now it so happened that I went forth and was absent one whole year; and when I returned from my journey I came to her by night, and saw a black slave lying with her; and they were talking, and dallying, and laughing, and kissing and playing the close-buttock game. When she saw me, she rose and came hurriedly at me with a gugglet of water; and, muttering spells over it, she besprinkled me and said, "Come forth from this thy shape into the shape of a dog," and I became on the instant a dog. She drove me out of the house, and I ran through the doorway nor ceased running until I came to a butcher's stall, where I stopped and began to eat what bones were there. When the stall-owner saw me, he took me and led me into his house, but as soon as his daughter had sight of me she veiled her face from me, crying out, "Dost thou bring men to me and dost thou come in with them to me?" ⟶ Her father asked, "Where is the man?" ⟶ And she answered, "This dog is a man whom his wife hath ensorcelled." ⟶ When her father heard her words, he said, "Allah upon thee, O my daughter, release him." ⟶ So she took a gugglet of water and, after uttering words over it, sprinkled upon me a few drops, saying, "Come forth from that form into thy former form." And I returned to my natural shape. Then I kissed her hand and said, "I wish thou wouldst transform my wife even as she transformed me." Thereupon she gave me some water, saying, "As soon as thou see her asleep, sprinkle this liquid upon her and speak what words thou heardest me utter, so shall she become whatsoever thou desirest." ⟶ I went to my wife and found her fast asleep; and, while sprinkling the water upon her, I said, "Come

forth from that form into the form of a mare-mule." So she became on the instant a she-mule, and she it is whom thou seest with thine eyes, O Sultan and head of the Kings of the Jann! ━━ Now when the old man had ceased speaking the Jinni shook with pleasure and ─ ─ And Shahrazad perceived the dawn of day and ceased saying her say. ━━ Then quoth Dunyazad, "O my sister, how pleasant is thy tale, and how tasteful; how sweet and how grateful!" ━━ She replied, "And what is this compared with that I could tell thee, the night to come, if the King spare me?" ━━ Then thought the King, "By Allah, I will not slay her until I hear the rest of her tale, for truly it is wondrous."

*When it was the Third Night*

Dunyazad said to her sister, "Finish for us that tale of thine," and she replied, "With joy and goodly gree!" ━━ It hath reached me, O auspicious King, that when the third old man told a tale to the Jinni more wondrous than the two preceding, the Jinni marvelled with exceeding marvel; and, shaking with delight, cried, "Lo! I have given thee the remainder of the merchant's punishment and for thy sake have I released him." ━━ Thereupon the merchant embraced the old men and thanked them, and these Shaykhs wished him joy on being saved and fared forth each one for his own city. ━━ "And yet, O King of the age, this tale is not more wondrous than another story I could tell." ━━ Asked the King, "What is this story?" ━━ And Shahrazad answered by relating the tale of

## THE PORTER AND THE THREE LADIES OF BAGHDAD

Once upon a time there was a Porter in Baghdad. It came to pass on a certain day, as he stood about the street leaning idly upon his crate, behold! there stood before him an honourable woman in a mantilla of silk, broidered with gold and bordered with brocade. She raised her face-veil and, showing two black eyes fringed with jetty lashes, said in the suavest tones, "Take up thy crate and follow me." The Porter was so dazzled he could hardly believe that he heard her aright, but he shouldered his basket in hot haste saying in himself, "O day of good luck! O day of Allah's grace!" and walked after her till she stopped at the door of a house. There she rapped, and presently came out to her an old man to whom she gave a gold piece, receiving from him in return strained wine clear as olive oil; and she set it safely in the hamper, saying "Lift and follow." He again hoisted up the crate and followed her. She then stopped at a fruiterer's shop and bought from him apples and quinces and peaches, and cucumbers of Nile growth, and limes and oranges and citrons, scented myrtle berries, Damascene nenuphars, flower of camomile, blood-red anemones, violets, and pomegranate-bloom. And she set the whole in the Porter's crate, saying "Up with it." So he lifted and followed her till she stopped at a butcher's booth and said, "Cut me off ten pounds of mutton." She paid him his price and he wrapped it in a banana-leaf, whereupon she laid it in the crate and said, "Hoist, O Porter." He hoisted, and followed her till she stopped at a grocer's, where she bought dry fruits and pistachio-kernels, raisins, shelled almonds and all wanted for dessert. At the confectioner's, she bought an earthen platter, and piled it with all kinds of sweetmeats, open-worked tarts and

fritters scented with musk, and lemon-loaves and melon-preserves, and "Zaynab's combs" and "ladies' fingers" and "Kazi's tit-bits" and goodies of every description; and she placed the platter in the Porter's crate. Then she stopped at a perfumer's and took from him ten sorts of waters. Of the greengrocer she bought pickled safflower and olives, in brine and in oil; with tarragon and cream-cheese and hard Syrian cheese; and she stowed them away in the crate, saying to the Porter, "Take up thy basket and follow me." ～ He went after her till she came to a fair mansion fronted by a spacious court, a tall, fine place to which columns gave strength and grace. The lady stopped at the door and knocked softly whilst the Porter stood behind her, thinking of naught save her beauty and loveliness. Presently the door swung back, and behold, there was a lady of tall figure, a model of beauty and loveliness, brilliance and symmetry and perfect grace. Her forehead was flower-white; her cheeks like the anemone ruddy bright; her eyes were those of the wild heifer or the gazelle, with eyebrows like the crescent-moon; her lips were coral-red, and her teeth like a line of strung pearls or of camomile petals. Her throat recalled the antelope's, and her breasts, like two pomegranates of even size, stood at bay as it were. ～ When the Porter looked upon her his wits were waylaid, and he said to himself, "Never have I in my life seen a day more blessed than this day!" Then quoth the lady-portress to the lady-cateress, "Come in from the gate and relieve this poor man of his load." So they went in and went on till they reached a spacious hall, built with admirable skill and beautified with all manner colours and carvings. In the midst stood a great basin full of water surrounding a fine fountain, and at the upper end on the raised dais was a couch of juniper-wood set with gems and pearls. Thereupon sat a lady bright of blee, whose eyes were fraught with enchantment and her eyebrows arched as for archery; her breath breathed ambergris and perfumery and her lips were sugar to taste and carnelian to see. ～ This third lady, the eldest, stepped forward with graceful swaying gait till she reached the middle of the saloon; and she and the cateress and the portress lifted the load from the Porter's head, emptying it of all that was therein and setting everything in its place. Lastly they gave him two gold pieces, saying "Wend thy ways, O Porter." But he went not, for he stood looking at the ladies and admiring what uncommon beauty was theirs, and their pleasant manners and kindly dispositions; and he gazed wistfully at that good store of wines and sweet-scented flowers and fruits and other matters. ◄━━ He marvelled with exceeding marvel and delayed his going; whereupon quoth the eldest lady, "What aileth thee that goest not; haply thy wage be too little?" And, turning to the cateress, she said, "Give him another dinar!" But the Porter answered, "By Allah, my lady, I wonder to see you single with ne'er a man about you and not a soul to bear you company. You want a fourth who shall be a person of good sense and prudence; smart witted, and one apt to keep careful counsel." ◄━━ His words pleased and amused them much; and they laughed at him and said, "Sit thee down and welcome to thee." But the eldest lady added, "By Allah, we may not suffer thee to join us save on one condition, and this is it: that no questions be asked as to what concerneth thee not." ◄━━ Answered the Porter, "I agree to this, O my lady, on my head and my eyes be it! ◄━━ Then arose the provisioneress, and she set the table by the fountain and put the flowers and sweet herbs in their jars, and strained the wine and ranged the flasks in a row, and made ready every requisite. Then sat she down, she and her sisters, placing amidst them the Porter, who kept deeming himself in a dream; and she took up the wine flagon, and poured out the first cup and drank it off, and likewise a second and a third. After this she filled a fourth cup which she handed to one of her sisters; and, lastly, she crowned a goblet and passed it to the Porter, and he stood up before the mistress of the house and said, "O lady, I am thy slave, thy Mameluke, thy white thrall, thy very bondsman." And they ceased not drinking (the Porter being in the midst of them) and dancing and laughing and singing ballads and ritornellos. All this time the Porter was carrying on with them, kissing,

toying, biting, handling; whilst one thrust a dainty morsel in his mouth, and another slapped him, and this cuffed his cheeks, and that threw sweet flowers at him; and he was in the very paradise of pleasure. ——— When the drink got the better of them, the portress stood up and doffed her clothes till she was mother-naked. However, she let down her hair about her body by way of shift and, throwing herself into the basin, disported herself and dived like a duck and swam up and down, and took water in her mouth and spurted it all over the Porter, and washed her limbs, and between her breasts, and inside her thighs, and all around her navel. Then she came up out of the cistern and, throwing herself on the Porter's lap and pointing to her solution of continuity, said, "O my lord, O my love, what callest thou this article?" ——— "I call that thy cleft," quoth the Porter. ——— She rejoined, "Wah! art thou not ashamed to use such a word?" and she caught him by the collar and soundly cuffed him. ——— Said he, "Thy vulva," and she struck him a second slap crying "O fie, this is another ugly word." ——— Quoth he, "Thy coynte," and she cried, "O thou! art wholly destitute of modesty?" and thumped him and bashed him. Then cried the Porter, "Thy clitoris," whereat the eldest lady came down upon him with a yet sorer beating, and said, "No." And the Porter went on calling the same commodity by sundry other names, but whatever he said they beat him more and more till his neck ached and swelled with the blows he had gotten. ——— At last he turned upon them asking "And what do you women call this article?" Whereto the damsel made answer, "The basil of the bridges," and the Porter cried thanks to Allah. ——— They passed round the cup and tossed off the bowl again, when the provisioneress stood up, and, stripping off all her clothes, cast herself into the cistern and did as the first had done. Then she came out of the water and, throwing her naked form on the Porter's lap and pointing to her machine, said, "O light of mine eyes, do tell me what is the name of this concern?" ——— He replied as before, "Thy slit," and she cuffed him and rejoined, "O fie! how canst thou say this without

blushing?" ⬥ He suggested, "The basil of the bridges," but she said, "No! no!" and struck him and slapped him. ⬥ Then he began calling out all the names he knew, and the girls kept on saying "No! no!" So he said, "I stick to the basil of the bridges." ⬥ And all the three laughed till they fell on their backs and laid slaps on his neck and said, "No! no! that is not its proper name." Thereupon he cried, "O my sisters, what is its name?" and they replied, "The husked sesame-seed." ⬥ After that time the eldest and handsomest lady stood up and stripped off her garments. Then she threw herself into the basin and swam and dived, sported and washed; and the Porter looked at her naked figure as though she had been a slice of the moon. Then the lady came up out of the basin and, seating herself upon his lap and knees, pointed to her genitory and said, "O my lordling, what be the name of this?" Quoth he, "The basil of the bridges," but she said, "Bah!" Quoth he, "The husked sesame," but she said, "Pooh!" Then said he, "Thy womb," and she cried, "Fie! art thou not ashamed of thyself?" And whatever name he gave declaring "'Tis so," she beat him and cried "No! no!" till at last he said, "O my sisters, and what is its name?" She replied, "It is entitled the Inn of Abu Mansur," whereupon the Porter again cried thanks to Allah. ⬥ At last the Porter rose up, and stripping off all his clothes, jumped into the tank and swam about and washed under his bearded chin and armpits, even as they had done. Then he came out and threw himself into the first lady's lap and rested his arms upon the lap of the portress and reposed his legs in the lap of the cateress and pointed to his prickle, and said, "O my mistresses, what is the name of this article?" All laughed at his words till they fell on their backs, and one said, "Thy pintle!" But he replied, "No!" and gave each one of them a bite by way of forfeit. ⬥ Then said they, "Thy pizzle!" but he cried, "No," and — — And Shahrazad perceived the dawn of day and ceased saying her say.

*When it was the Fourth Night*

Quoth Dunyazad, "Finish for us thy story," and Shahrazad answered, "With joy and goodly gree." ⬥ It hath reached me, O auspicious King, that the damsels stinted not saying to the Porter "Thy prickle, thy pintle, thy pizzle," and he ceased not kissing and biting and hugging until his heart was satisfied, and they laughed on till they could no more. At last one said, "O our brother, what, then, is it called?" "Its veritable name," said he, "is mule Burst-all, which browseth on the basil of the bridges, and muncheth the husked sesame, and nighteth in the Inn of Abu Mansur."

⬥ Then laughed they till they fell on their backs, and returned to their carousal, and ceased not to be after this fashion till night began to fall. Thereupon said the three ladies to the Porter, "Up and on with those sorry old shoes of thine and turn thy face and show us the breadth of thy shoulders!" ⬥ Said he, "By Allah, to part with my soul would be easier for me than departing from you." ⬥ Said the procuratrix, "Suffer him to tarry with us, that we may laugh at him, for surely he is a right merry rogue and a witty." So they said, "Thou must not remain with us this night save on condition that thou submit to our commands, and that whatso thou seest, thou ask no questions thereanent, nor enquire of its cause." ⬥ "All right," rejoined he, and they said, "Go read the writing over the door." So he rose and went to the entrance and there found written in letters of gold: WHOSO SPEAKETH OF WHAT CONCERNETH HIM NOT, SHALL HEAR WHAT PLEASETH HIM NOT! ⬥ Then the cateress arose and set food before them and they ate; after which she lighted the lamps and candles and burned ambergris and set on fresh fruit and the wine service, when they fell to carousing and they ceased not to eat and drink and chat, nibbling dry fruits and laughing and playing tricks for the space of a full hour when lo! a knock was heard at the gate. One of them rose and went to see what it was and presently returned, saying "Truly our pleasure for this night is to be perfect. At the gate be three Persian

Kalandars with their beards and heads and eyebrows shaven; and all three blind of the left eye — which is surely a strange chance. They have just entered Baghdad, and the cause of their knocking at our door is simply because they cannot find a lodging. And, O my sisters, each of them is a figure o' fun after his own fashion; and if we let them in we shall have matter to make sport of." She gave not over persuading them till they said to her, "Let them in, and make thou the usual condition with them that they speak not of what concerneth them not, lest they hear what pleaseth them not." ⁓ So she rejoiced and going to the door presently returned with the three Monoculars whose beards and mustachios were clean shaven. The three ladies welcomed them and wished them joy of their safe arrival. Then they sat together, and the portress served them with drink; and, as the cup went round merrily, quoth the Porter, "And you, O brothers mine, have ye no story or rare adventure to amuse us withal?" They called for musical instruments; and the portress brought them a tambourine and a lute and a harp; and each mendicant took one and tuned it and struck up a merry tune while the ladies sang so lustily that there was a great noise. And whilst they were carrying on, behold! some one knocked at the gate, and the portress went to see what was the matter there. ⁓ Now the cause of that knocking, O King (quoth Shahrazad), was this: the Caliph, Harun al-Rashid, had gone forth from the palace, as was his wont now and then, to see and hear what new thing was stirring. He was in merchant's gear, and he was attended by Ja'afar, his Wazir, and by Masrur, his Sworder of Vengeance. As they walked about the city, their way led them towards the house of the three ladies, where they heard the loud noise of musical instruments and singing and merriment; so quoth the Caliph to Ja'afar, "I long to enter this house and hear those songs and see who sing them. Contrive some pretext for our appearing among them." Ja'afar replied, "I hear and I obey," and knocked at the door, whereupon the portress came out and opened. Then Ja'afar came forward and kissing the ground before her said, "O my lady, we be

merchants from Tiberias-town. Haply of your kindness and courtesy you will suffer us to tarry with you this night, and Heaven will reward you!" The portress looked upon them and seeing them dressed like merchants and men of grave looks and solid, she opened the door to them. And the Caliph entered followed by Ja'afar and Masrur; and when the girls saw them they stood up to them in respect and made them sit down and looked to their wants, saying "Welcome, and well come and good cheer to the guests, but with one condition! Speak not of what concerneth you not, lest ye hear what pleaseth you not." "Even so," said they; and sat down to their wine and drank deep. ～～ When the wine gat the better of them, the eldest lady who ruled the house rose and took the cateress by the hand, and said, "Rise, O my sister, and let us do that which we must do." Then the portress stood up and proceeded to remove the table-service and the remnants of the banquet; and renewed the pastiles and cleared the middle of the saloon. Then she called the Porter, and said, "How scanty is thy courtesy! now thou art no stranger; nay, thou art one of the household." ～～ "What would ye I do?" ～～ "Come help me." ～～ So he went to help her and saw two black bitches with chains round their necks; and she said to him, "Take hold of them," and he took them and led them into the middle of the saloon. Then the eldest lady tucked up her sleeves above her wrists and, seizing a scourge, said to the Porter, "Bring forward one of the bitches." He brought her forward, dragging her by the chain, and the lady ceased not beating her till her forearm failed her. Then, casting the scourge from her hand, she pressed the bitch to her bosom and, wiping away her tears with her hands, kissed her head. Then she said to the Porter, "Take her away and bring the second," and she did with her as she had done with the first. ～～ Now the heart of the Caliph was touched at these cruel doings; his chest straitened and he lost all patience in his desire to know why the two bitches were so beaten. ～～ The procuratrix then entered a closet and brought out of it a bag of satin with green fringes and two tassels of gold. She drew out from the bag a lute which she tuned by tightening its pegs; and when it was in perfect order, she began to sing. When the portress heard the song she cried out "Alas! Alas!" and rent her raiment, and fell to the ground fainting; and the Caliph saw on her back the welts of the whip, and marvelled with exceeding wonder. Then the procuratrix arose and sprinkled water on her and brought her a fresh and very fine dress and put it on her. ———The Caliph said to Ja'afar, "Didst thou not see the scars upon the damsel's body? I cannot keep silence or be at rest till I learn the truth of her condition and the story of this other maiden and the secret of the two black bitches." But Ja'afar answered, "O our lord, they made it a condition with us that we speak not of what concerneth us not." ———Then said the portress, "By Allah, O my sister, come to me and complete this service for me." Replied the procuratrix, "With joy and goodly gree," so she took the lute, and leaned it against her breasts and swept the strings with her finger-tips, and began singing. ———Now when the portress heard her second ode she shrieked aloud and tore her garments, as she did the first time, and fell to the ground fainting. Thereupon the procuratrix rose and brought her a second change of clothes after she had sprinkled water on her. ———The provisioneress again turned to the lute and began to sing. When the portress heard the third song she cried aloud and rent her garments down to the very skirt and fell to the ground fainting a third time, again showing the scars of the scourge. ———Then said the three Kalandars, "Would Heaven we had never entered this house, for verily our visit hath been troubled by sights which cut to the heart." ———The Caliph asked, "Why so? Are ye not of the household?" and quoth they, "No; nor indeed did we ever set eyes on the place till within this hour." ———Hereat the Caliph marvelled and rejoined, "This man who sitteth by you, would he not know the secret of the matter?" So they questioned the Porter, but he replied, "Never in my born days did I darken these doors till to-day and my companying with them was a curious matter." ———Then said the Caliph, "We be

seven men, and they only three women without even a fourth to help them; so let us question them of their case; and, if they answer us not, fain we will be answered by force." All of them agreed to this except Ja'afar, and then words ran high and talk answered talk, and they disputed as to who should first put the question, and at last all fixed upon the Porter. ━━◆━━ And as the jingle increased the house mistress could not but notice it and asked them, "O ye folk! on what matter are ye talking so loudly?" Then the Porter stood up respectfully before the lady of the house and said, "O my lady, this company earnestly desire that thou acquaint them with the story of the two bitches and what maketh thee punish them so cruelly; and then thou fallest to weeping over them and kissing them; and they want to hear the tale of thy sister and why she hath been bastinado'd with palm-sticks. These are the questions they charge me to put, and peace be with thee." ━━◆━━ When she heard these words she cried, "By Allah, ye have wronged us, O our guests, with grievous wronging; for when you came before us we made compact and condition with you, that whoso should speak of what concerneth him not should hear what pleaseth him not." Then she struck the floor thrice with her

hand crying, "Come ye quickly," and lo! a closet door opened and out of it came seven negro slaves with drawn swords in hand to whom she said, "Pinion me those praters' elbows and bind them each to each." They did her bidding and asked her, "O veiled and virtuous! is it thy command that we strike off their heads?" but she answered, "Leave them that I may question them before their necks feel the sword."⟶ "By Allah, O my lady!" cried the Porter, "slay me not for others' sin; all these men offended and deserve the penalty of crime save myself. For our night had been charming till the appearance of these monocular Kalandars."— — And Shahrazad perceived the dawn of day and ceased to say her say.

*When it was the Fifth Night*

She spoke on. It hath reached me, O auspicious King, that the lady, after laughing at the Porter despite her wrath, accosted the three Kalandars and asked them, "Are ye brothers?" and they answered, "No, by Allah." Then quoth she to one among them, "Wast thou born blind of one eye?" and quoth he, "No, by Allah, 'twas a marvellous matter and a wondrous mischance which caused my eye to be torn out."⟶ She questioned the second and the third; but all replied like the first. Thereupon she turned towards them and said, "Let each and every of you tell me his tale and explain the cause of his coming to our place; and if his story please us let him wend his way."⟶ The first to come forward was the Porter, who said, "O my lady, I am a man and a porter. This dame, the cateress, hired me to carry a load and took me first to the shop of a vintner, then to the booth of a butcher; thence to the stall of a fruiterer; thence to a grocer who also sold dry fruits; thence to a confectioner and a perfumer-cum-druggist and from him to this place where there happened to me with you what happened. Such is my story and peace be on us all!" At this the lady laughed and said, "Rub thy head and wend thy ways!" but he cried, "By Allah, I will not stump it till I hear the stories of my companions." ⟶ Then came forward one of the Monoculars and began to tell her

THE FIRST KALANDAR'S TALE

Know, O my lady, that my father was a King and he had a brother who was a King over another city; and it came to pass that I and my cousin were both born on one and the same day. And years and days rolled on, and as we grew up I used to spend certain months with him. Now my cousin and I were sworn friends, and one day he said to me, "O my cousin, I have a great service to ask of thee." And I replied, "With joy and goodly gree." Then he left me; but after a little while he returned leading a lady veiled and richly apparelled with ornaments worth a large sum of money, and said, "Take this lady with thee and go before me to such a burial ground and enter with her into such a sepulchre and there await my coming." ———— The oaths I swore to him made me keep silence and suffered me not to oppose him; so I led the woman to the cemetery and both I and she took our seats in the sepulchre; and hardly had we sat down when in came my uncle's son. He went straight to the tomb in the midst of the sepulchre and, breaking it open with an adze, set the stones on one side; then he fell to digging till he came upon a large iron plate, and on raising it there appeared below it a staircase vaulted and winding. The lady at once went down by the staircase and disappeared. ———— Then quoth he to me, "O son of my uncle, when I shall have descended into this place, restore the trap-door and heap back the earth upon it, and then mix this unslaked lime with water and plaster the outside so that none looking upon it shall say: 'This is a new opening in an old tomb.'" And he went down the stairs and disappeared. ———— When he was lost to sight I replaced the iron plate and did all his bidding till the tomb became as it was before. I slept that night without seeing my uncle;

and, when the morning dawned, I remembered the scenes of the past evening and I repented of having obeyed my cousin when penitence was of no avail. So I went out to the grave-yard and sought for the tomb under which he was, but could not find it; and I ceased not wandering about from sepulchre to sepulchre, and tomb to tomb, but I could not find the tomb I sought. I mourned over the past, and remained in my mourning seven days, and I found no way to dispel my grief save travel and return to my father. ──── But as I was entering my father's capital a crowd of rioters sprang upon me and pinioned me. I wondered thereat with all wonderment and questioned those that bound me of the cause of their doing. One of them said to me, "Fortune has been false to thy father; his troops betrayed him and the Wazir who slew him now reigneth in his stead and we lay in wait to seize thee by the bidding of him." ──── Now between me and the usurper there was an olden grudge, the cause of which was this: one day, as I was standing on the terrace-roof of the palace, a bird lighted on the top of the Wazir's house when he happened to be there. I shot at the bird and missed the mark; but I hit the Wazir's eye and knocked it out. Now the Wazir could not say a single word, for that my father was King of the city; but he hated me everafter. So when I was set before him hand-bound and pinioned, he straightway gave orders for me to be beheaded. I asked, "For what crime wilt thou put me to death?" whereupon he answered, "What crime is greater than this?" pointing the while to the place where his eye had been. Quoth I, "This I did by accident," and quoth he, "If thou didst it by accident, I will do the like by thee with intention." And he thrust his finger into my left eye and gouged it out. Then he put me into a chest and said to the sworder, "Take charge of this fellow, and go off with him to the waste lands about the city; then draw thy scymitar and slay him, and leave him to feed the beasts and birds." ──── So the headsman fared forth with me and when he was in the midst of the desert, he took me out of the chest and cried, "O my lord, fly for thy life and nevermore return to this land." Hardly believing in my escape, I kissed his hand and thought the loss of my eye a light matter in consideration of my escaping from being slain. ◥I arrived at my uncle's capital; and, going in to him, told him of what had befallen my father and myself; whereat he wept with sore weeping and would have applied certain medicaments to my eye, but he saw that it was become as a walnut with the shell empty. Then said he, "O my son, better to lose eye and keep life!" ◥After that I could no longer remain silent about my cousin, who was his only son and one dearly loved, so I told him all that had happened, and I and my uncle went to the grave-yard and looked right and left, till at last I recognised the tomb and we both rejoiced with exceeding joy. We entered the sepulchre and loosened the earth about the grave; then, upraising the trap-door, descended some fifty steps till we came to the foot of the staircase when lo! we were stopped by a blinding smoke. We advanced again till we came upon a saloon, whose floor was strewed with flour and grain and provisions and all manner necessaries; and in the midst of it stood a canopy sheltering a couch. Thereupon my uncle found his son and the lady, lying in each other's embrace; but they had become black as charred wood. When my uncle saw this spectacle, he spat in his son's face and said, "Thou hast thy deserts, O thou hog! this is thy judgement in the transitory world, and yet" — — And Shahrazad perceived the dawn of day and ceased saying her say.

*When it was the Sixth Night*

Shahrazad continued. It hath reached me, O auspicious King, that the Kalandar thus went on with his story: My uncle struck his son with his slipper, and I marvelled at his hardness of heart and said, "By Allah, O my uncle, calm thy wrath: dost thou not see how horrible it is that naught of him remaineth but a black heap of charcoal? And is not that enough, but thou must smite him with thy slipper?" ◥Answered he, "O son of my brother, this youth from his boyhood was madly in love with his own sister; and when they grew up sin befel between them; and, although I could hardly believe it, I confined him and chided him and threatened him with the severest threats. After that I lodged them apart and shut her up. ———"Now when my son saw that I separated them, he secretly built this souterrain and furnished it and transported to it victuals; and, when I had gone out a-sporting, came here with his sister and hid from me. Then His righteous judgement fell upon the twain and consumed them with fire from Heaven." ——— Then he wept and I wept and he looked at me and said, "Thou art my son in his stead." Then we mounted the steps and, after restoring the tomb to its former condition, we returned to the palace. But hardly had we sat down ere we heard the tomtoming of the kettle-drum and tantara of trumpets, and the rattling of lances, and the clamours of assailants, and the neighing of steeds. We were amazed and learned that the Wazir who usurped my father's kingdom had come down upon us with armies like the sands of the sea. They attacked the city unawares; and the citizens, being powerless to oppose them, surrendered: my uncle was slain and I made away. ———I could think of no way to escape save by shaving off my beard and my eyebrows. So I shore them off and, changing my fine clothes for a Kalandar's rags, I fared forth from my uncle's capital and made for this city, hoping that some one would assist me to the presence of the Prince of the Faithful, and the Caliph who is the Viceregent of Allah that I might tell him my tale. I arrived here this very night, when I saw this second Kalandar; so I salam'd to him saying, "I am a stranger!" and he answered, "I too am a stranger!" And as we were conversing behold! up came our companion, this third Kalandar. Then we three walked on till darkness overtook us and Destiny drave us to your house. Such, then, is the cause of the shaving of my beard and mustachios and eyebrows; and the manner of my losing my eye. ———All marvelled much at this tale and the lady of the house said, "Rub thy head and wend thy ways," but he replied, "I will not go, till I hear the history of the two others." ———Thereupon the second Kalandar came forward; and, kissing the ground, began to tell

## THE SECOND KALANDAR'S TALE

Know, O my lady, that I was not born one-eyed. I am a King, son of a King, and was brought up like a Prince. I exercised myself in all branches of learning until I surpassed the people of my time and my fame was bruited abroad over all climes and cities. Amongst others the King of Hind heard of me and sent to my father to invite me to his court, with offerings and presents and rarities. So we put to sea and sailed till we made the land. Then, after loading the camels with our presents for the Prince, we set forth. But we had marched only a little way, when behold! fifty horsemen, ravening lions to the sight, set upon us and I fled after I had gotten a wound, a grievous hurt. ⟐ I went forth unknowing whither I went, and I fared on until I came to the crest of a mountain where I took shelter for the night in a cave. When day arose I set out again, nor ceased after this fashion till I arrived at a fair city. ⟐ I was glad of my arrival for I was wearied with the way, but I knew not whither to betake me. So I accosted a Tailor sitting in his little shop and saluted him; he returned my salam, and bade me kindly welcome and asked me of the cause of my strangerhood. I told him all from first to last, and he said, "O youth, disclose not thy secret to any: the King of this city is the greatest enemy thy father hath, and thou hast cause to fear for thy life." Then he set meat and drink before me; and I ate and drank and he with me; and we conversed till night-fall, when he cleared me a place in a corner of his shop and brought me a carpet and a coverlet. I tarried with him three days, at the end of which time he bought me an axe and a rope and gave me in charge to certain wood-cutters. With these guardians I went forth into the forest, where I cut fuel-wood the whole of

my day and came back in the evening bearing my bundle on my head. I sold it for half a dinar, with part of which I bought provision and laid by the rest. In such work I spent a whole year and when this was ended I went out one day, as was my wont, into the wilderness; and, wandering away from my companions, I chanced on a thickly grown lowland in which there was an abundance of wood. So I entered and I found the gnarled stump of a great tree and loosened the ground about it and shovelled away the earth. Presently my hatchet rang upon a copper ring; so I cleared away the soil and behold! the ring was attached to a wooden trap-door. This I raised and there appeared beneath it a staircase. I descended the steps and came to a door, which I opened, and I found myself in a noble hall strong of structure and beautifully built, where was a damsel like a pearl of great price. She looked at me and said, "Art thou man or Jinni?" "I am a man," answered I. "Now who brought thee to this place where I have abided five-and-twenty years without yet seeing man in it?" Quoth I, "O my lady, my good fortune led me hither for the dispelling of my cark and care." Then I related to her all my mishap from first to last, and my case appeared to her exceeding grievous; so she wept and said, "I will tell thee my story. I am the daughter of the King Ifitamus, lord of the Islands of Abnus, who married me to my cousin. But on my wedding night an Ifrit snatched me up and set me down in this place, whither he conveyed all I needed of fine stuffs, raiment and jewels and furniture, and meat and drink and other else. Once in every ten days he comes here and lies a single night with me, then wends his way, and he hath agreed with me that if ever I need him by night or by day, I have only to pass my hand over yonder two lines engraved upon the alcove and he will appear. And, as there remain six days before he come again, wilt thou abide with me and go hence the day before his coming?" I replied "Yes, and yes again!" Hereat she was glad and, springing to her feet, seized my hand and carried me through an arched doorway to a Hammam-bath, a fair hall and richly decorate. I doffed my clothes, and she doffed hers; then we bathed and when we felt cool after the bath, she set food before me and we ate and sat at converse and carousal till nightfall and with her I spent the night — such night never spent I in all my life! On the morrow delight followed delight till I had lost my wits and said, "Come, O my charmer, and I will deliver thee from the spell of thy Jinni." She laughed and replied, "Content thee and hold thy peace: of every ten days one is for the Ifrit and the other nine are thine." Quoth I (and in good sooth drink had got the better of me), "This very instant will I break down the alcove whereon is graven the talisman and summon the Ifrit that I may slay him!" When she heard my words her colour waxed wan and she said, "By Allah, do not!" But I paid no heed to her words, nay! I raised my foot and administered to the alcove a mighty kick — — And Shahrazad perceived the dawn of day and ceased to say her say.

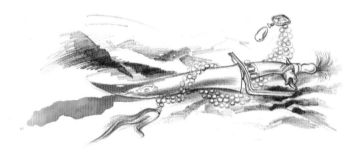

*When it was the Seventh Night*

She spoke. It hath reached me, O auspicious King, that the second Kalandar thus continued: But when, O my mistress, I kicked that alcove with a mighty kick, behold! the air starkened and darkened and thundered and lightened. And the damsel cried, "The Ifrit is upon us! By Allah, thou hast brought ruin upon me; but fly for thy life and go up by the way thou camest down!" So I fled up the staircase; but, in the excess of my fear, I forgot sandals and hatchet. And when I had mounted two steps I turned to look for them, and lo! I saw the earth cleave asunder, and there arose from it a monster of hideousness who said to the damsel, "What mishap hath betided thee?" ～ "No mishap hath befallen me," she answered, "save that my heart was heavy with sadness so I drank a little wine to hearten myself; then I rose to obey a call of Nature, but the wine had gotten into my head and I fell against the alcove." ～ "Thou liest, like the whore thou art! What be these axe and sandals but the belongings of some mortal who hath been in thy society?" ～ She answered, "I never set eyes upon them till this moment." ～ Quoth the Ifrit, "These words are absurd, thou strumpet!" Then he stripped her naked and bound her hands and feet and set about torturing and trying to make her confess. ～ I climbed the stair on the quake with fear; and I replaced the trap-door and covered it with earth. Then repented I of what I had done and thought of the lady and her beauty and loveliness, and the tortures she was suffering at the hands of the accursed Ifrit, and how all that had happened to her was for the cause of me. So I wept bitterly. ～ Then I walked till I reached the home of my friend, the Tailor, and retired to my corner. Here I sat pondering and musing on what had befallen me, when behold, the Tailor came to me and said, "O youth, in the shop there is an old man who seeketh thee: he hath thy hatchet and thy sandals which the woodcutters recognised and directed him to thee." When I heard these words I turned yellow with fear and, before I could recover myself, lo! the floor clove asunder, and out of it rose the Ifrit. ～ He snatched me up as a hawk snatcheth a mouse and flew high in air; but presently descended and plunged with me under the earth and set me down in the subterranean palace wherein I had passed that blissful night. And there I saw the lady stripped to the skin, her limbs bound to four stakes and blood welling from her sides. The Ifrit covered her person and said, "O wanton, is not this man thy lover?" ～ She looked upon me and replied, "I wot him not nor have I ever seen him before this hour!" ～ Quoth the Ifrit, "If thou know him not, take this sword and strike off his head." ～ She hent the sword in hand and came close up to me. Then, O my mistress, the lady threw away the

sword and said, "How shall I strike the neck of one I wot not and who hath done me no evil? Such deed were not lawful in my law!" and she held her hand. ———— Said the Ifrit, " 'Tis grievous to thee to slay thy lover; and, because he hath lain with thee, thou endurest these torments and obstinately refusest to confess." Then he turned to me and asked me, "O man, haply thou also dost not know this woman?" whereto I answered, "And pray who may she be? assuredly I never saw her till this instant." ———— "Then take the sword," said he, "and strike off her head and I will believe that thou wottest her not and will leave thee free to go." I took the sword and raised my hand to smite, but she signed to me with her eyebrows: "Have I failed thee in aught of love; and is it thus that thou requitest me?" I understood what her looks implied and my eyes filled with tears to overflowing and I cast the sword from my hand saying "O mighty Ifrit, how can it be lawful for me, a man, to smite her neck whom I never saw in my whole life? I cannot do such misdeed though thou cause me drink the cup of death and perdition." ———— Then said the Ifrit, "Ye twain show the good understanding between you; but I will let you see how such doings end." He took the sword, and struck off the lady's hands first, and then her feet; and she farewelled me with her dying eyes. Then he turned to me and said, "O mortal, we have it in our law that, when the wife committeth adultery it is lawful for us to slay her. But as for thee I am not well satisfied that thou hast wronged me in her. Nevertheless, I must not let thee go unharmed; so ask a boon of me and I will grant it." ———— "What boon shall I crave of thee?" ———— "Ask me this boon: into what shape I shall bewitch thee; wilt thou be a dog, or an ass or an ape?" I rejoined, "By Allah, spare me!" and I humbled myself before him with exceeding humility. ———— He replied, "Talk me no long talk, it is in my power to slay thee; but I give thee instead thy choice." ———— Quoth I, "O thou Ifrit, it would besit thee to pardon me even as the Envied pardoned the Envier." ———— Quoth he, "And how was that?" And I began to tell him

## THE TALE OF THE ENVIER AND THE ENVIED

They relate, O Ifrit, that in a certain city were two men who dwelt in adjoining houses, having a common wall; and one of them envied the other and did his utmost to injure him; and his malice at last grew on him till he could hardly eat or enjoy the sweet pleasures of sleep. But the Envied did nothing save prosper; and the more the other strove to injure him, the more the Envied got and gained and throve. At last the malice of his neighbour and the man's constant endeavour to work him a harm came to his knowledge; so he repaired to another city where he bought himself a piece of land in which was a dried up draw-well, old and in ruinous condition. Here he built him an oratory and took up his abode therein, and devoted himself to prayer; and Fakirs and holy mendicants flocked to him from all quarters; and his fame went abroad through the city and that country-side. ━━ Presently the news reached his envious neighbour of what good fortune had befallen him, so he travelled to the place and presented himself at the holy man's hermitage, and was met by the Envied with welcome and greeting and all honour. Then quoth the Envier, "I wish to give thee a piece of good news; so come with me to thy cell." Accordingly they set out and walked a little way until the twain reached the ruinous old well. And as they stood upon the brink the Envier gave the Envied a push which tumbled him headlong into it, unseen of any; whereupon the Envier fared forth, and went his ways, thinking to have had slain his neighbour. ━━ Now this well happened to be haunted by the Jann, who bore the Envied up and let him down little by little, till he reached the bottom. Then one of them asked his fellows, "Wot ye who be this man?" and they answered, "Nay." ━━ "This man," continued the speaker, "is the Envied who,

flying from the Envier, came to dwell in our city, and here founded this holy house; but the Envier cunningly contrived to deceive him and cast him into the well where we now are. But the fame of this good man hath come to the Sultan of our city who designeth to visit him on the morrow on account of his daughter." ～— "What aileth his daughter?" asked one, and another answered, "She is possessed of a spirit; but, if this pious man knew the remedy, her cure would be as easy as could be." —～ Hereupon one of them inquired, "And what is the medicine?" and the other replied, "The black tom-cat which is with him in the oratory hath, on the end of his tail, a white spot; let him pluck seven white hairs from the spot, then let him fumigate her therewith and the spirit will flee from her and not return." ～— All this took place, O Ifrit, within earshot of the Envied who listened readily. When dawn broke the Envied climbed up the wall of the well. Then he plucked the seven tail-hairs from the white spot of the black tom-cat and laid them by him; and hardly had the sun risen ere the Sultan entered the hermitage. The Envied gave him a hearty welcome, and seating him by his side asked him, "Shall I tell thee the cause of thy coming?" ～— The King answered, "Yes." —～ "Thou hast come upon pretext of a visitation; but it is in thy heart to question me of thy daughter. Send and fetch her, and I trust to heal her forthright." ～— The King in great joy sent for his daughter, and they brought her pinioned and fettered. The Envied sat her down behind a curtain and taking out the seven hairs fumigated her therewith; whereupon that which was in her head cried out and departed from her. The Sultan rejoiced with a joy that nothing could exceed, and kissed his daughter's eyes and the holy man's hand; and he married him to her and the Envied thus became son-in-law to the King. ～— And after a little the Wazir died and the King said, "Whom can I make Minister in his stead?" ～— "Thy son-in-law," replied the courtiers. So the Envied became a Wazir. ～— And after a while the Sultan died and the lieges said, "Whom shall we make King?" and all cried, "The Wazir." So the

Wazir was forthright made Sultan. ━━━ One day as he had mounted his horse and was riding amidst his Emirs and Wazirs and the Grandees of his realm his eye fell upon his old neighbour, the Envier, so he turned to one of his Ministers, and said, "Bring hither that man and cause him no affright." The Wazir brought him and the King said, "Give him a thousand miskals of gold from the treasury, and load him ten camels with goods for trade, and send him under escort to his own town." Then he bade his enemy farewell and sent him away and forbore to punish him for the many and great evils he had done. ━━━ See, O Ifrit, the mercy of the Envied to the Envier, who had hated him from the beginning and had borne him such bitter malice and — — ━━━ Said the Ifrit, "Lengthen not thy words! As to my slaying thee fear it not, as to my pardoning thee hope it not; but from my bewitching thee there is no escape." Then he tore me from the ground and flew with me into the firmament. Presently he set me down on a mountain, and taking a little dust, over which he muttered some magical words, sprinkled me therewith, saying, "Quit that shape and take thou the shape of an ape!" And on the instant I became a tail-less baboon. ━━━ Now when he had left me and I saw myself in this ugly and hateful shape, I wept for myself, but resigned my soul to the tyranny of Time and Circumstance. I descended the mountain and found at the foot a desert plain, over which I travelled for the space of a month till my course brought me to the brink of the briny sea. After standing there awhile, I was ware of a ship in the offing. I waited till the ship drew near, and I leaped on board. I found her full of merchants and passengers and one of them cried, "O Captain, this ill-omened brute will bring us ill-luck!" and another said, "Let us kill it!" and another said, "Slay it with the sword!" and yet another, "Drown it!" But I sprang up and laid hold of the Captain's skirt, and shed tears which poured down my chops. The Captain took pity on me, and said, "O merchants! this ape hath appeared to me for protection and I will protect him; so let none do him aught hurt or harm." Then he entreated me kindly and whatsoever he said I understood,

91

and ministered to his every want and served him as a servant, so that he came to love me. ⁓ The vessel sailed on for the space of fifty days; at the end of which we cast anchor under the walls of a great city wherein was a world of especially learned men. No sooner had we arrived than we were visited by certain Mameluke-officials from the King of that city; who, after boarding us, greeted the merchants and giving them joy of safe arrival said, "Our King welcometh you, and sendeth you this roll of paper, whereupon each and every of you must write a line. For ye shall know that the King's Minister, a calligrapher of renown, is dead, and the King hath sworn a solemn oath that he will make none Wazir in his stead who cannot write as well as he could." ⁓ Each of the merchants who knew how to write wrote a line on the scroll; after which I stood up and snatched the roll out of their hands. They tried to stay me and scare me, but I signed to them that I could write, whereat all marvelled and the Captain cried, "Let him write; and if he scribble and scrabble we will kick him out and kill him; but if he write fair and scholarly I will adopt him as my son; for surely I never yet saw a more intelligent and well-mannered monkey than he. Would Heaven my real son were his match in morals and manners." ⁓ I took the reed and, stretching out my paw, dipped it in ink and wrote couplets, in letters large and small, and in hands from the simplest to the most formal. Then I gave the scroll to the officials and they carried it before the King. When he saw the paper no writing pleased him save mine; and he said to the assembled courtiers, "Go seek the writer of these lines and dress him in a splendid robe of honour; then mount him on a she-mule, let a band of music precede him and bring him to the presence." At these words they smiled and said, "O King, thou orderest us to bring to thy presence the man who wrote these lines. Now the truth is that he who wrote them is an ape, a tail-less baboon, belonging to the ship-captain." The King marvelled at their words and shook with mirth and said, "I am minded to buy this ape of the Captain. Not the less, do you clothe him in the robe of honour and mount him on the mule and let him be surrounded

by the guards and preceded by the band of music." ⁓ They came to the ship and carried me in state-procession through the streets; and came all agog crowding to gaze at me, and the town was astir and turned topsy-turvy on my account. ⁓ When they brought me up to the King and set me in his presence, I kissed the ground before him three times, and he bade me be seated, and I sat respectfully on shins and knees, and all who were present marvelled at my fine manners. Thereupon he ordered the lieges to retire; and, when none remained save the King's majesty, the Eunuch on duty and a little white slave, he bade them set before me the table of food, containing all manner of birds. Then he signed me to eat with him; so I rose and kissed ground before him, then sat me down and ate with him. The King then said to his Eunuch, "O Mukbil, go to thy mistress, Sitt al-Husn, and say to her, 'Come, speak the King who biddeth thee hither to take thy solace in seeing this right wondrous ape!'" So the Eunuch went out and presently returned with the lady who, when she saw me veiled her face and said, "O my father! hast thou lost all sense of honour? How cometh it thou art pleased to send for me and show me to strange men?" ⁓ "O Sitt al-Husn," said he, "no man is here save this little foot-page and the Eunuch who reared thee and I, thy father. From whom, then, dost thou veil thy face?" ⁓ She answered, "This whom thou deemest an ape is a young man, a clever and polite, a wise and learned and the son of a King; but he is ensorcelled by the Ifrit Jirjaris, who is of the seed of Iblis." ⁓ The King marvelled at his daughter's words and, turning to me, said, "Is this true that she saith of thee?" and I signed by a nod of my head the answer, "Yea, verily," and wept sore. ⁓ "O my daughter," said her father, "I conjure thee, by my life, disenchant this young man, that I may make him my Wazir and marry thee to him, for indeed he is an ingenious youth and a deeply learned." ⁓ "With joy and goodly gree," she replied and, — — And Shahrazad perceived the dawn of day and ceased saying her say.

Shahrazad continued. It hath reached me, O auspicious King, that the Kalandar continued thus: O my lady, the King's daughter hent in hand a knife whereon were inscribed Hebrew characters and described a wide circle in the midst of the palace-hall, and therein wrote in Cufic letters mysterious names and talismans; and she uttered words and muttered charms, and lo! the Ifrit presented himself in his own shape and aspect. His hands were like many-pronged pitch-forks, his legs like the masts of great ships, and his eyes like cressets of gleaming fire. The King's daughter cried at him, "No welcome to thee, O dog!" whereupon he changed to the form of a lion and said, "O traitress, how is it thou hast broken the oath we sware that neither should contraire other!" "O accursed one," answered she, "how could there be a compact between me and the like of thee?" Said he, "Take what thou has brought on thyself." The lion opened his jaws and rushed upon her; but she was too quick for him; and plucking a hair from her head, waved it in the air muttering over it; and the hair straightway became a trenchant sword-blade, wherewith she cut the lion in twain. Then the two halves flew away in air and the head changed to a scorpion and the Princess became a serpent, and the two fought, coiling and uncoiling, a stiff fight. Then the scorpion changed to a vulture and the serpent became an eagle which set upon the vulture, and hunted him till he became a black tom-cat, which miauled and grinned and spat. Thereupon the eagle changed into a pie-bald wolf and these two battled in the palace when the cat, seeing himself overcome, changed into a worm and crept into a huge red pomegranate. The pomegranate swelled to the size of a watermelon in air and broke to pieces, and all the grains fell out and were scattered about till they covered the whole floor. Then the wolf became a snow-white cock, which fell to picking up the grains; but by doom of destiny one seed rolled to the fountain-edge and there lay hid. The cock fell to crowing and clapping his

wings till he saw the grain which had rolled to the fountain edge, and rushed eagerly to pick it up when behold! it sprang into the midst of the water and became a fish and dived to the bottom of the basin. Thereupon the cock changed to a fish, and plunged in after the other, and the two disappeared for a while and lo! we heard loud shrieks and cries of pain which made us tremble. After this the Ifrit rose out of the water, and he was as a burning flame. And the Princess likewise came forth from the basin and she was one live coal of flaming lowe; and these two, she and he, battled for the space of an hour, until their fires entirely compassed them about and their thick smoke filled the palace. ➤ Suddenly, the Ifrit yelled out from under the flames and blew fire in our faces. The damsel overtook him and breathed blasts of fire at his face, and the sparks from her and from him rained down upon us and her sparks did us no harm. But one of his sparks alighted upon my eye and destroyed it, making me a monocular ape; and another fell on the King's face, scorching the lower half, burning off his beard and mustachios and causing his under teeth to fall out; while a third alighted on the Castrato's breast, killing him on the spot. So we despaired of life and made sure of death when lo! the Princess burnt the Ifrit, and he was become a heap of ashes. ➤ Then she came up to us and said, "Reach me a cup of water." They brought it to her and she spoke over it words we understood not, and sprinkling me with it cried, "By virtue of the Truth, and by the Most Great name of Allah, I charge thee return to thy former shape." And behold! I became a man as before, save that I had utterly lost an eye. ➤ Then she cried out, "The fire! The fire! O my dear papa, an arrow from the accursed has wounded me to the death. I had no trouble till the time when the pomegranate burst and the grains scattered, but I overlooked the seed wherein was the very life of the Jinni. Had I picked it up his death would have been swift and final; but as Fate and Fortune decreed, I saw it not and there befel between him and me a sore struggle. But Destiny willed that my cunning prevail over his cunning; and I burned him to death. As for me I am a dead woman." And we looked at her and saw naught but a heap of ashes by the side of the heap that had been the Ifrit. We mourned for her and I wished I had been in her place, but there is no gainsaying the will of Allah. When the King saw his daughter's terrible death, he plucked out what was left of his beard and beat his face and rent his raiment, and cried, "O youth! Would to Heaven we had never seen thee, for we took pity on thee and thereby on thy account I first lost my daughter who to me was well worth an hundred men. Secondly I have suffered that which befel me by reason of the fire and the loss of my teeth, and my Eunuch also was slain. I blame thee not: the doom of Allah was on thee as well as on us and thanks be to the Almighty for that my daughter delivered thee, albeit thereby she lost her own life! Go forth now, O my son, from this my city; and if I ever see thee again I will surely slay thee." So I went forth from his presence, O my lady, weeping bitterly. And I shaved my poll and beard and mustachios and eyebrows, and cast ashes on my head and donned the coarse black robe of a Kalandar. Then I fared forth; and every day I pondered all the calamities which had betided me, and I wept. I journeyed through many regions and saw many a city, intending for Baghdad that I might seek audience, in the House of Peace, with the Commander of the Faithful and tell him all that had befallen me. I arrived here this very night and found this first Kalandar, and presently up came this third Kalandar, and so we all three walked on together, none of us knowing the other's history, till Destiny drave us to this door. Said the house-mistress, "Thy tale is indeed a rare; so rub thy head and wend thy ways," but he replied, "I will not budge till I hear my companions' stories." Then came forward the third Kalandar, and said, "O illustrious lady! my history is not like that of these my comrades, but more wondrous and far more marvellous. In their case Fate and Fortune came down on them unawares; but I drew down destiny upon my own head and brought sorrow on mine own soul, and shaved my own beard and lost my own eye. Hear then

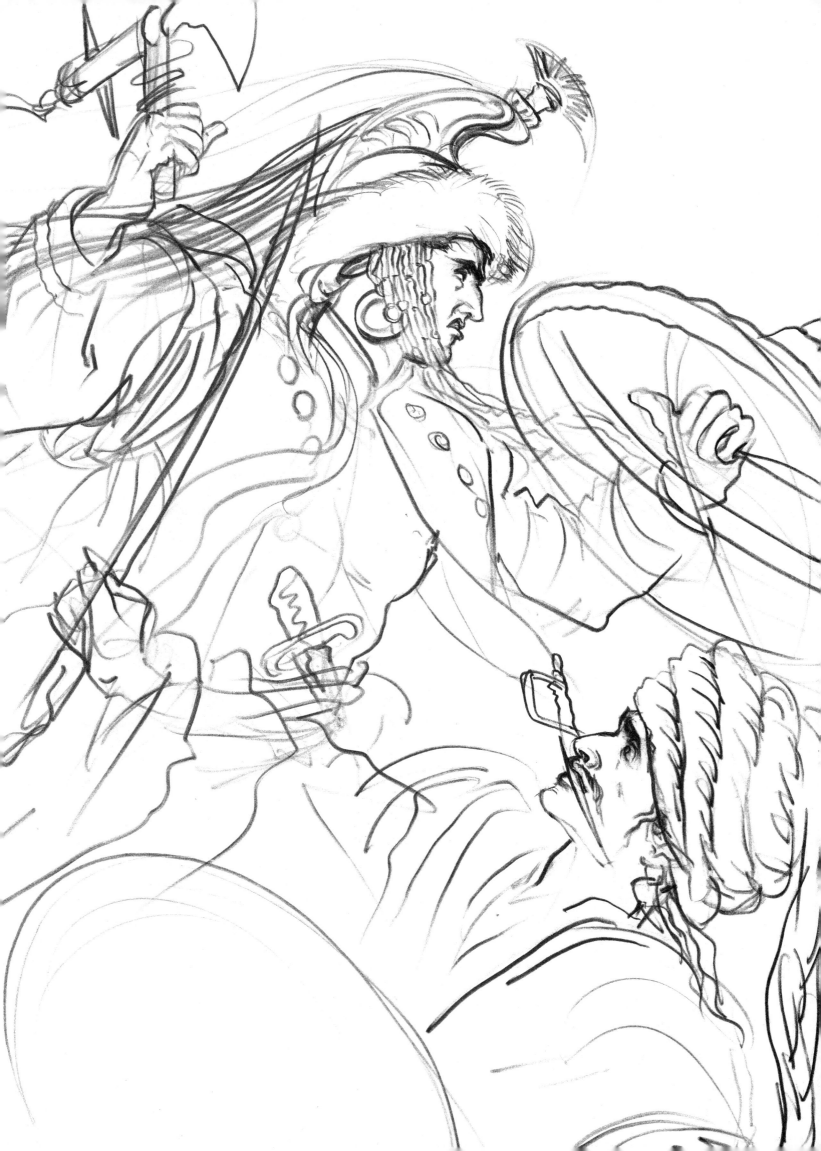

## THE THIRD KALANDAR'S TALE

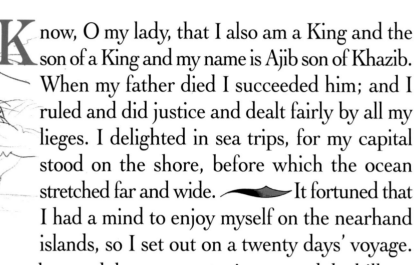

Know, O my lady, that I also am a King and the son of a King and my name is Ajib son of Khazib. When my father died I succeeded him; and I ruled and did justice and dealt fairly by all my lieges. I delighted in sea trips, for my capital stood on the shore, before which the ocean stretched far and wide. ———It fortuned that I had a mind to enjoy myself on the nearhand islands, so I set out on a twenty days' voyage.

But one night a wind struck us and the sea rose against us and the billows sorely buffetted us and a dense darkness settled round us. We prayed to Allah and besought Him; but the storm-blasts ceased not to blow against us nor the surges to strike us till morning broke, when the seas sank to mirrory stillness. Presently we made an island where we took our rest for several days. Then we set out again and we found ourselves in strange waters, where the Captain lost his reckoning, so said we to the look-out man, "Get thee to the mast-head and keep thine eyes open." He swarmed up the mast and cried aloud, "I espy to starboard something dark, very like a fish floating on the face of the sea, and to larboard there is a loom in the midst of the main, now black and now bright." When the Captain heard the look-out's words he plucked out his beard and beat his face and he fell to weeping and all of us wept for his weeping and I said, "O Captain, tell us what it is the look-out saw." ———"O my Prince," answered he, "know that the currents carry us willy-nilly to a mountain of black stone, hight the Magnet Mountain. As soon as we are under its lea, every nail in plank will fly out and cleave fast to the mountain, for Al-mighty Allah hath gifted the loadstone with a mysterious virtue and a love for iron. The bright spot upon its summit is a dome of brass, vaulted upon

ten columns; and on its crown is a horseman who rideth a horse of brass and holdeth a lance of brass; and there hangeth on his bosom a tablet of lead graven with names and talismans." Then, O my lady, the Captain wept with exceeding weeping and each and every one of us farewelled his friend and charged him with his last will and testament in case he might be saved. ———In the morning we found ourselves much nearer the Loadstone Mountain, and the nails flew out and all the iron in them sought the Magnet Mountain and clove to it like a network; so that by the end of the day we were all struggling in the waves round about the mountain. Some of us were saved, but more were drowned and as for me, O my lady, the wind and waters threw me at the feet of the Mountain. There I found a practicable path leading by steps carven out of the rock to the summit — — And Shahrazad perceived the dawn of day and ceased to say her say.

*When it was the Ninth Night*

She continued. It hath reached me, O auspicious King, that the third Kalandar said on to the lady. ———I breasted the ascent, clinging to the steps and notches hewn in the stone, and mounted little by little. And the Lord stilled the wind and aided me. I fell asleep under the dome and heard in my dream a mysterious Voice saying, "O son of Khazib! when thou wakest from thy sleep dig under thy feet and thou shalt find a bow of brass and three leaden arrows. Take the bow and shoot the arrows at the horseman on the dome-top and free mankind from this sore calamity. When thou hast shot him he shall fall into the sea. This done, there will appear a skiff carrying a man of brass (other than he thou shalt have shot) holding a pair of paddles. Do thou embark with him, but beware of naming Allah Almighty. He will row thee for ten days, till he bring thee to certain islands called the Islands of Safety, and thence thou shalt easily reach a port and find those who will convey thee to thy native land." ———Then I started up from my sleep in joy and gladness and, hastening to do the bidding of the mysterious Voice, found the bow and arrows

and shot at the horseman and tumbled him into the main. Nor had I long to wait ere I saw a skiff in the offing coming towards me and, when the skiff came up to me, I saw therein a man of brass; and I embarked without uttering a word. The boatman rowed on with me through the first day and the second and the third, in all ten whole days, till I caught sight of the Islands of Safety; whereat I joyed with exceeding joy and for stress of gladness exclaimed, "Allah, Allah!" The skiff forthwith upset and cast me upon the sea. ⬧ I swam the whole day, until my forearms and shoulders were numbed with fatigue and I felt like to die. Yet the sea was still surging and presently there came a billow and, bearing me up high in air, threw me on dry land. ⬧ I was pondering my case and longing for death when behold! I saw a ship making for the island; so I clomb a tree and hid myself. Presently the ship anchored and landed ten slaves, who walked on till they reached the middle of the island. Here they dug deep into the ground, until they uncovered a plate of metal which they lifted, thereby opening a trap-door. After this they returned to the ship and thence brought bread and flour, honey and fruits, clarified butter, leather bottles containing liquors and many household stuffs; also furniture, table-service, rugs, and carpets; in fact, all needed to furnish a dwelling. After this the slaves again went on board and brought back with them garments as rich as may be, and in the midst of them came an old, old man, of whom very little was left. And the Shaykh held by the hand a youth cast in beauty's mould, all elegance and perfect grace; so fair that his comeliness deserved to be proverbial. ⬧ All went down by the trap-door and did not reappear for an hour, or rather more; at the end of which time the slaves and the old man came up without the youth and, replacing the iron plate and carefully closing the door-slab as it was before, they returned to the ship and made sail. I came down from the tree and scraped off and removed the earth from the trap-door; and when I lifted it up it disclosed a winding staircase of stone. At this I marvelled and, descending the steps, I found a fair hall spread with various kinds of carpets and silk stuffs, wherein was a youth sitting upon a raised couch and leaning back on a round cushion; but he was alone. When he saw me he turned pale; but I said, "Calm thy fears; no harm shall come near thee; I am a man like thyself whom Destiny hath sent to bear thee company in thy loneliness. But now tell me, what causeth thee to dwell thus in solitude under the ground?" When he was assured that I was no Jinni, he rejoiced, and he said, "O my brother, my story is a strange story. ⁓ "My father is a merchant-jeweller possessed of great wealth, but he was not blessed with a child. Now on a certain night he dreamed a dream that he should be favoured with a son, who would be short-lived. On the following night my mother conceived and when her time was fulfilled she bare me; whereat my father rejoiced and made banquets and called together the neighbors and fed the Fakirs and the poor. Then he assembled the astrologers and astronomers and the wizards and wise ones of the time; and they drew out my birth scheme and said to my father, 'Thy son shall live to fifteen years, but in his fifteenth there is a sinister aspect. Fifty days after the rider that standeth on the Magnet Mountain shall fall from his steed thy son will die, and his slayer will be he who shoots down the horseman, a Prince named Ajib son of King Khazib.' ⁓ "Ten days ago news came to him that the horseman had fallen into the sea and my father, being in mortal fear for me, set me in this place under the earth; and when forty days shall have gone by without danger to me, he will come and take me away; for he hath done all this only in fear of Prince Ajib. Such, then, is my story and the cause of my loneliness." ⁓ When I heard his history I marvelled and said in my mind, "I am the Prince Ajib who hath done all this; but as Allah is with me I will surely not slay him!" We ate and drank and sat talking till the greater part of the night was gone, when he lay down to rest and I covered him up and went to sleep myself. Next morning I arose and brought him warmed water wherewith he washed his face and he said to me, "Heaven requite thee for me with every blessing, O youth! By Allah, if I get quit of this danger I will make my father reward thee and

send thee home healthy and wealthy; and, if I die, then my blessing be upon thee." I answered, "May the day never dawn on which evil shall betide thee!" Then I set before him food, and we ate; and I got ready perfumes for the hall, wherewith he was pleased. We played and ate sweetmeats and we played again and took our pleasure till nightfall, when I rose and lighted the lamps, and sat telling him stories till the hours of darkness were far spent. Then he lay down to rest and I covered him up and rested also. ⬥ And thus I continued to do, O my lady, and affection for him took root in my heart, and I said to myself, "The astrologers lied when they predicted that he should be slain by Ajib bin Khazib: by Allah, I will not slay him." I ceased not ministering to him and conversing and carousing with him for thirty-nine days. ⬥ On the fortieth night the youth rejoiced and said, "Praise be to Allah — who hath preserved me from death! O my brother, cut me up a water-melon, and sweeten it with a little sugar-candy." So I went to the store-room and bringing out a fine water-melon, set it on a platter, saying, "O my master, hast thou not a knife?" ⬥ "Here it is," answered he, "upon the high shelf." So I got up in haste and drew the knife from its sheath; but my foot slipped and I fell and the knife buried itself in the youth's heart. He died on the instant. ⬥ When I saw that I had slain him, I cried out with a loud and bitter cry and beat my face and rent my raiment and said, "What dire misfortune is this! What a disaster! What an affliction! O Allah mine, I implore thy pardon and declare to Thee" — — And Shahrazad perceived the dawn of day and ceased to say her say.

*When it was the Tenth Night*

Shahrazad spoke on. ⬥ It hath reached me, O auspicious King, that Ajib thus continued his tale to the lady: When I was certified that I had slain him, I arose and, ascending the stairs, replaced the trap-door and covered it with earth. Then I looked out seawards and saw the ship making for the island. So I climbed up into a high tree and concealed myself; and hardly had I done so when the slaves and the ancient man, the youth's father, made direct for the place. They found the youth lying at full length, and the knife deep in his heart, and at the sight they shrieked and wept and beat their faces, loudly cursing the murderer. ⬥ At last they carried the slain youth up and covered him with a shroud of silk. Whilst they were making for the ship the old man sobbed a single sob and his soul fled his flesh. The slaves shrieked aloud and showered dust on their heads and redoubled their weeping and wailing. They then carried their dead master to the ship side by side with his dead son and set sail. ⬥ Then, O my lady, I wandered every day round about the island, and every night I returned to the underground hall. Thus I lived for a month, till at last I observed that the sea showed a passage of dry land to the west. So I arose and got me to the main land, where I beheld a fire from afar burning with a blazing light. So I made for it, hoping haply to find succour. ⬥ When I drew near the fire aforesaid, lo! it was a palace with gates of copper which gleamed and glistened from afar showing what had seemed to me a fire. I sat down against the gate, but I was hardly settled before there met me a Shaykh, an old, old man, and ten young men clothed in sumptuous gear and all were blind of the left eye which appeared as plucked out. They saluted me with the Salam and asked me of my history; whereupon I related all what had befallen me. Marvelling at my tale, they took me to the mansion, where each of the youths took his seat on his own couch and the old man seated himself upon a smaller one in the middle of the hall, saying to me, "O youth, sit thee down and ask not of our case nor of the loss of our eyes." Presently he rose up and, entering a closet, disappeared, but presently returned bearing ten trays each covered with a strip of blue stuff. He set a tray before each youth and, lighting ten wax candles, he stuck one upon each tray, and drew off the covers and lo! under them was naught but ashes and powdered charcoal and kettle soot. Then all the young men fell a-weeping and wailing, and they blackened their faces and buffetted their brows and beat their breasts and they ceased not till dawn drew nigh. Now when I saw this, O my lady, I could not keep silence, so I said to them, "Why stint ye to tell me your history, and the cause of your losing your eyes and your blackening your faces with ashes and soot?" Hereupon they turned to me and said, "O young man, question us no questions." Then they slept and I slept and when they awoke the old man brought us food; and we sat conversing and carousing till the noon of night, when the old man rose and brought them the trays of soot and ashes. And they did as they had done on the preceding night, nor more, nor less. I abode with them after this fashion for the space of a month during which time they used to blacken their faces with ashes every night, and to wash and change their raiment when the morn was young. At last, I lost command of myself, for my heart was aflame with fire unquenchable and I said, "O young men, will ye not acquaint me with the reason of thus blackening your faces?" Quoth they, "'Twere better to keep these things secret." Still I was bewildered, and quoth I to them, "There is no help for it: ye must acquaint me with what is the reason of these doings." Thereupon they said, "Remember, O youth, that should ill befal thee we will not again harbour thee nor suffer thee to abide amongst us." Bringing a ram they slaughtered it and skinned it, then they gave me a knife saying, "Take this skin and stretch thyself upon it and we will sew it around thee. Presently there shall come to thee a certain bird, the Roc, that will catch thee up and then set thee down near a palace. When thou feelest he is no longer flying, rip open the pelt with this blade and come out of it. The bird will be scared and will fly away. Enter the palace and thou shalt win to thy wish; for we have all entered there, and such is the cause of our losing our eyes and of our blackening our faces." I rejoiced at their words and they did with me as they said; and the Roc bore me off and set me down by the palace. The door stood open as I entered and I found myself in a spacious hall. At the upper end of the hall I saw forty damsels, sumptuously dressed and one and all bright as moons.

When they saw me the whole bevy came up to me and said, "Welcome and well come and good cheer to thee, O our lord!" Then they made me sit down upon a high divan and one of them set meat before me, and I ate and they ate with me and we conversed till nightfall, when five of them arose and laid the trays and spread them with flowers and fragrant herbs and fruits and confections in profusion. ⁓ Such gladness possessed me that I forgot the sorrows of the world till the time came for our rest, when they said, "O our lord, choose from amongst us her who shall be thy bed-fellow this night and not lie with thee again till forty days be past." So I chose a girl fair of face and perfect in shape, with eyes Kohl-edged by nature's hand; 'twas as if she were some limber graceful branchlet or the slender stalk of sweet basil to amaze and to bewilder man's fancy. I lay with her that night, and none fairer I ever knew. ⁓ When it was morning, the damsels bathed me and robed me in fairest apparel. Then we ate and drank and the cup went round till nightfall, when I chose from among them one fair of form and face, soft-sided and a model of grace. ⁓ To be brief, O my mistress, I remained with them in all solace and delight of life, every night lying with one or other of them. But at the head of the new year they came to me, weeping and crying and clinging about me; whereat I wondered and said, "What may be the matter? verily you break my heart!" And they answered, "O our lord and master, thou art the cause of our tears. Know that we are the daughters of Kings, who have lived together for years; and once in every year we are perforce absent for forty days. We are about to depart, and we fear lest thou disobey our injunctions. Here now we commit to thee the keys of the palace, which containeth forty chambers, and thou mayest open of these thirty and nine, but beware lest thou open the fortieth door, for therein is that which shall separate us for ever." ⁓ Quoth I, "By Allah I will never open that fortieth door, never and no wise!" ⁓ Thereupon all departed, flying away like birds and leaving me alone in the palace. ⁓ When evening drew near I opened the door of the first chamber and found myself in a garden with trees of freshest green and ripe fruits of yellow sheen; and its birds were singing clear and keen, and rills ran wimpling through the fair terrene. The sight and sounds brought solace to my sprite; and I walked among the trees. I looked then upon the quince and inhaled its fragrance. Then I went out of the place and locked the door as it was before. ⬥ When it was the morrow I opened the second door and found myself in a spacious plain set with tall date-palms and watered by a running stream whose banks were shrubbed with bushes of rose and jasmine, while eglantine, violet and lily, and the winter gilliflower carpeted the borders; and their delicious odours filled my soul with delight. After taking my pleasure there awhile I went from it and opened the third door wherein I saw a high open hall hung with cages full of birds which made sweet music. My heart was filled with pleasure thereby; and I slept in that aviary till dawn. I gave not over opening place after place until nine and thirty days were passed and in that time I had entered every chamber except that one whose door the Princesses had charged me not to open. But my thoughts, O my mistress, ever ran on that forbidden fortieth. Nor had I patience to forbear, and I opened the door which was plated with red gold, and entered. I was met by a perfume so sharp and subtle that it made my senses drunken as with strong wine. ⬥ This was a chamber whose floor was bespread with saffron and blazing with light. Presently, O my lady, I espied a noble steed, black as the murks of night when murkiest, standing ready saddled and bridled, and his saddle was of red gold. When I saw this I marvelled and led the steed without the palace and mounted him. But he would not stir from his place. So I hammered his sides with my heels, but he moved not. ⬥ Then I took the rein-whip and struck him withal. When he felt the blow, he neighed a neigh with a sound like deafening thunder and, opening a pair of wings, flew up with me in the firmament of heaven far beyond the eyesight of man. After a full hour of flight he descended and alighted on a terrace roof and, shaking me off his back, lashed me on the face with his tail and gouged out

my left eye. Then he flew away. ━━━━◆━━━━ I went down from the terrace and found myself amongst the ten one-eyed youths. Quoth I, "Behold I have become one like unto you," and quoth they, "Thou shalt not sojourn with us and now get thee hence!" and they drove me away. ━━━━◆━━━━ Then I shaved beard and mustachios and eye-brows, and wandered in Kalandar-garb till I arrived at Baghdad. Here I met these two other Kalandars standing bewildered; so I saluted them saying, "I am a stranger!" and they answered, "And we likewise be strangers!" By the freak of Fortune we were like to like, three Kalandars and all blind of the left eye. ━━━━◆━━━━ Such, O my lady, is the cause of the shearing of my beard and the manner of my losing an eye. Said the lady to him, "Rub thy head and wend thy ways," but he answered, "By Allah, I will not go until I hear the stories of the others." ━━━━◆━━━━ Then the lady, turning towards the Caliph and Ja'afar and Masrur, said to them, "Do ye also give an account of yourselves, you men!" Whereupon Ja'afar told her their story, and she said, "I grant you your lives each for each sake, and now away with you all." ━━━━◆━━━━ On the dawn of the next morning, Harun al-Rashid sat upon the throne of his sovereignty; and, turning to Ja'afar, he said, "Bring me the three ladies and the two bitches and the three Kalandars." So Ja'afar brought them all before him. Then the Minister turned to them and said in the Caliph's name, "We pardon you your maltreatment of us and your want of courtesy, in consideration of the kindness which forewent it, and for that ye knew us not. Now however I would have you to know that ye stand in presence of Harun al-Rashid. Speak ye therefore before him the truth and the whole truth!" When the ladies heard Ja'afar's words, the eldest came forward and — — And Shahrazad perceived the dawn of day and ceased to say her say.

*When it was the Eleventh Night*

She spoke. It hath reached me, O auspicious King, that the eldest lady stood forth before the Commander of the Faithful and began to tell

## THE ELDEST LADY'S TALE

Verily mine is a strange tale. Yon two black bitches are my eldest sisters by one mother and father; and these two others are my sisters by another mother. When my father died, each took her share of the heritage, and after a while my mother also deceased. In due course of time my sisters married with the usual festivities and lived with their husbands and set out on their travels together. Thus they threw me off. ———My brothers-in-law deserted my sisters in foreign parts and after five years my eldest sister returned to me with her clothes in rags and tatters, and truly she was in the foulest and sorriest plight. I sent her to the bath and dressed her in a suit of mine own, and boiled for her a bouillon and brought her some good wine and said to her, "O my sister, my circumstances are easy, for I have made much money by spinning and cleaning silk; and I and you will share my wealth alike." I entreated her with all kindliness and she abode with me a whole year, during which our thoughts and fancies were always full of our other sister. Shortly after she too came home in yet fouler and sorrier plight than that of my eldest sister; and I dealt by her still more honourably than I had done by the first. ———After a time they said to me, "O our sister, we desire to marry again," and I replied, "O eyes of me! now-a-days good men and true are become rarities and curiosities, and ye have already made trial of matrimony and have failed." But they would not accept my advice and they married without my consent. ———In a little time their husbands played them false, and thereupon they came to me in abject case and made their excuses to me and said, "Take us back as thy handmaidens that we may eat our mouthful." And I took them in and redoubled my kindness

to them. ◄━━► We ceased not to live after this loving fashion for a full year, when I resolved to sell my wares abroad. So I said to my sisters, "Will ye abide at home whilst I travel, or would ye prefer to accompany me on the voyage?" ◄━━► "We will travel with thee," answered they, "for we cannot bear to be parted from thee." ◄━━► So I divided my monies into two parts, one to accompany me and the other to be left in charge of a trusty person, for, as I said to myself, "Haply some accident may happen to the ship and yet we remain alive; in which case we shall find on our return what may stand us in good stead." I took my two sisters and we went a-voyaging some days and nights; but the master was careless and the ship went astray and entered a sea other than the sea we sought. ◄━━► So we landed in a strange city, and we saw at the gate men hending staves in hand; but when we drew near them, behold! they had become stones. Then we entered the city and found all who therein woned into black stones enstoned, and we said, "Doubtless there is some mystery in all this." Then we dispersed. ◄━━► I went up to the King's palace and found the King himself seated in the midst of his Chamberlains and Nabobs and Emirs and Wazirs. I drew nearer and saw him sitting on a throne inlaid with pearls and gems; and his robes were adorned with jewels of every kind. Around him stood fifty Mamelukes, but when I drew near to them lo! all were black stones. I walked on and entered the great hall of the Harem, and here I saw the Queen arrayed in robes purfled with fresh young pearls, and on her head a diadem, and around her neck hung collars and necklaces; but she had been turned into a black stone. ◄━━► Presently I espied an open door for which I made straight and found leading to it a flight of seven steps. So I walked up and came upon a closet whose door stood ajar. Then peeping through a chink I considered the place and lo! it was an oratory wherein was a prayer-niche with two wax candles burning and lamps hanging from the ceiling. In it was spread a prayer-carpet whereupon sat a youth fair of face and rare of form, in brief a sweet, a sugar-stick; and before him on its stand was a

copy of the Koran, from which he was reading. ——I glanced at him
with one glance of eyes, and my heart was at once taken captive-wise; so I
asked him, "O my lord and my love, tell me what hath befallen the people
of this city, and what was the reason of thy escaping their doom." And he
answered, "Hearing is obeying! Know, O handmaid of Allah, that this
city was the capital of my father who is the King thou sawest on the throne
transfigured by Allah's wrath to a black stone, and the Queen thou foundest
in the alcove is my mother. They and all the people of the city were Magians
who fire adored in lieu of the Omnipotent Lord. Now it so fortuned that
there was with us an old woman, who, inwardly believing in Allah and
His Apostle, conformed outwardly with the religion of my people; and my
father placed thorough confidence in her. So when I was well-nigh grown
up my father committed me to her charge saying: 'Take him and teach him
the rules of our faith.' So she took me and taught me the tenets of Al-
Islam, and she said to me: 'O my son, keep this matter concealed from thy
sire and reveal naught to him lest he slay thee.' ——"The people of
the city redoubled the error of their ways; until one day, behold, they
heard a loud and terrible sound and a crier crying out with a voice like
roaring thunder, 'O folk of this city, leave ye your fire-worshipping and
adore Allah the All compassionate King!' At this, fear and terror fell upon
the citizens and they crowded to my father and asked him, 'What is this
awesome voice we have heard, for it hath confounded us with the excess
of its terror?' and he cautioned them, 'Let not a voice shake your steadfast
sprite nor turn you back from the faith which is right.' Their hearts in-
clined to his words and they ceased not to worship the fire. A full year
from the time they heard the first voice there came a second cry. Still they
persisted in their malpractices till one day the wrath of Heaven descended
upon them with all suddenness, and all were metamorphosed into black
stones, and none was saved save myself. ——"From that day I am
constant in prayer and fasting and reading and reciting the Koran; but I
am indeed grown weary by reason of my loneliness, having none to bear

me company." ﹏ Then said I to him (for in very sooth he had won my heart), "O youth, wilt thou fare with me? And know that she who standeth in thy presence will be thy handmaid? Indeed my life was no life before it fell in with thy youth, for it was fated that we should meet." And I ceased not to use every art till he consented. — — And Shahrazad perceived the dawn of day and ceased to say her permitted say.

*When it was the Twelfth Night*

She continued. It hath reached me, O auspicious King, that the lady slept that night lying at the youth's feet and hardly knowing where she was for excess of joy. ﹏ As soon as the next morning dawned (the eldest lady pursued, addressing the Caliph), I arose and we went down side by side from the castle to the city, where we were met by the Captain and my sisters and slaves who had been seeking for me. When they saw me they rejoiced, and I told them all I had seen and related the story of the young Prince and the transformation wherewith the citizens had been justly visited. Hereat all marvelled, but when my two sisters (these two bitches, O Commander of the Faithful!) saw me by the side of my young lover, they jaloused me on his account and plotted mischief against me. ﹏ We went on board rejoicing and soon we had exchanged the sea of peril for the seas of safety. But after we had retired to rest and were sound asleep, my two sisters arose and took me up, bed and all, and threw me into the sea: they did the same with the young Prince who, as he could not swim, sank and was drowned. As for me, would Heaven I had been drowned with him, but Allah deemed that I should be saved; so He threw in my way a piece of timber which I bestrided, and the waves tossed me to and fro till they cast me upon an island coast, a high land and an uninhabited. I walked about the island the rest of the night and, when morning dawned, I saw a rough track barely fit for child of Adam to tread, leading to what proved a shallow ford connecting island and main land. As soon as the sun had risen I set out along the foot-track and ceased not walking till I reached the main land. ━━━ Now when there remained between me and the city but a two hours' journey behold! a great serpent came fleeing towards me in all haste. She was pursued by a Dragon who overtook her and seized her by the tail, whereat her tears streamed down and her tongue was thrust out in her agony. I took pity on her and, picking up a stone, threw it at the Dragon's head with such force that he died then and there; and the serpent, opening a pair of wings, disappeared from before my eyes. I sat down marvelling over that adventure, but I was weary and I slept. ━━━ When I awoke I found a jet-black damsel sitting at my feet, and by her side stood two black bitches. I asked her, "O my sister, who and what art thou?" and she answered, "How soon hast thou forgotten me! I am the serpent whom thou didst just now deliver from the Dragon. I am a Jinniyah and he was a Jinn who hated me, and as soon as thou freedest me from him I flew on the wind to the ship whence thy sisters threw thee, and I transformed thy two sisters into these black bitches, for I know all that hath passed between them and thee. Now (continued the serpent that was), I swear by all engraven on the seal-ring of Solomon (with whom be peace!), unless thou deal to each of these bitches three hundred stripes every day I will come and imprison thee forever under the earth." I answered, "Hearkening and obedience!" and away she flew. ━━━ Since then I have never failed, O Commander of the Faithful, to beat them with that number of blows till their blood flows, and well they wot that their being scourged is no fault of mine. And this is my tale and my history! ━━━ The Caliph marvelled at her adventures and then signed to Ja'afar who said to the Portress, "And thou, how camest thou by the welts and wheals upon thy body?" So she began

Know, O Commander of the Faithful, that I had a father who deceased and left me great store of wealth. I presently married one of the richest of his day. I abode with him a year when he also died. Thus I became passing rich and my reputation spread far and wide. One day as I was sitting at home, behold! there came in to me an old woman with cheeks sucked in, and eyes rucked up, and eyebrows scant and scald, and head bare and bald; her teeth were broken by time, back bent, and face blotched, and rheum running, and hair like a snake black-and-white-speckled, in complexion a very fright. The old woman salamed to me and said, "I have at home an orphan daughter and this night is her wedding. We be poor folks and strangers in this city. So do thou earn for thyself a recompense and a reward in Heaven by being present." So pity gat hold on me and I said, "Hearing is consenting." At this the old woman rejoiced and bowed her head to my feet and kissed them, saying, "Allah requite thee weal and comfort thy heart even as thou hast comforted mine!" So I threw on my mantilla and, making the old crone walk before me and my handmaidens behind me, I fared till we came to a street well watered and swept neat, where the breeze blew cool and sweet. Here we were stopped by a gate arched over with a dome of marble stone firmly seated on solidest foundation and leading to a Palace whose walls from earth rose tall and proud, and whose pinnacle was crowned by the clouds. The old woman knocked and the gate was opened to us. We passed on till we entered a saloon, whose like for grandeur and beauty is not to be found in this world. It was hung with silken stuffs and was illuminated with branches,

sconces and tapers ranged in double row, an avenue abutting on the upper end of the saloon, where stood a couch of juniper-wood encrusted with pearls. Hardly had we taken note of this when there came forth a young lady more perfect than the moon when fullest, with a favour brighter than the dawn gleaming with saffron-hued light. The fair young girl said to me, "Welcome and well come to my sister, the dearly-beloved, and a thousand greetings!" Then sat she down and said to me, "O my sister, I have a brother: he is a youth handsomer than I, and he hath fallen desperately in love with thee. He hath given silver to this old woman that she might visit thee and bring me in company with thee, for he is fain to marry thee." When I heard these words and saw myself fairly entrapped in the house, I said, "Hearing is consenting." She was delighted at this and clapped her hands; whereupon a door opened and out of it came a young man blooming in the prime of life, exquisitely dressed, a model of beauty and loveliness and symmetry and perfect grace, with gentle winning manners and eye-brows like a bended bow and shaft on cord, and eyes which bewitched all hearts with sorcery lawful in the sight of the Lord. When I looked at him I loved him; and the young lady again clapped her hands and behold! a side-door opened and out of it came the Kazi with his four assessors as witnesses. They saluted us and drew up the marriage-contract between me and the youth and retired. Then the youth turned to me and said, "O my lady, I have a condition to lay on thee." Quoth I, "O my lord, what is that?" "Swear thou wilt never look at any other than myself nor incline thy body or thy heart to him." I swore readily enough to this and he joyed with exceeding joy. When night did come he led me to the bride-chamber and slept with me on the bed and continued to kiss and embrace me till the morning — such a night I had never seen in my dreams. I lived with him a life of happiness and delight for a full month, at the end of which I asked his leave to go to the bazar and he gave me permission. So I donned my

mantilla and, taking with me the old woman, I went to the silk-mercers, where the old woman said to the young merchant, "Show this lady the most costly stuffs thou hast," and he replied, "Hearkening and obedience!" As she began to sound his praise, I said sharply to her, "We want nought of thy sweet speeches. Our wish is to buy of him whatsoever we need, and return home."——— So he brought me all I sought and I offered him his money, but he refused to take it. Then quoth I to the old woman, "If he will not take the money, give him back his stuff." "By Allah," cried he, "not a thing will I take from thee: I sell it not for gold or for silver, but I give it all for a single kiss."——— Asked the old woman, "What harm will it do thee if he get a kiss from thee?"———Replied I, "Knowest thou not that I am bound by an oath?"———But she answered, "Now whist! just let him kiss thee, and no harm shall befal thee." And she ceased not to persuade me and make light of the matter till evil entered into my mind and, declaring I would ne'er consent, consented. So I veiled my eyes and held up the edge of my mantilla between me and the people passing and he put his mouth to my cheek under the veil. But while kissing me he bit me a bite so hard that it tore the flesh from my cheek. The old woman caught me in her arms and said to me, "Come, let us go home before the matter become public and thou be dishonoured. And when thou art safe inside the house feign sickness and cover thyself up; and I will bring thee powders and plasters, and thy wound will be healed at the latest in three days."——— When it was night my husband came in to me and I said, "I am not well: my head acheth badly." Then he lighted a candle and looked hard at me and asked, "What is that wound I see on thy cheek and in the tenderest part too? Thou hast been false to thine oath!"——— He cried out with a loud cry, whereupon a door opened and in came seven black slaves whom he commanded to drag me from my bed and throw me down in the middle of the room. One of them pinioned my elbows, and a second sat upon my knees. Drawing his sword, he gave it to a third and said, "Strike her and cut her in twain and let each one take half and cast it

into the Tigris that the fish may eat her. Such is the retribution due to those who violate their vows and are unfaithful to their love." And he redoubled in wrath, when the old woman rushed in and threw herself at my husband's feet and kissed them and wept and said, "O my son, by the rights of my fosterage and by my long service to thee, I conjure thee pardon this young lady, for indeed she hath done nothing deserving such doom." And she ceased not to weep and importune him till he relented and said, "I pardon her, but needs must I set on her my mark which shall show upon her all her life." ⬩⬩⬩ Then he bade the slaves drag me along the ground and lay me out at full length; and when the slaves had so sat upon me that I could not move, he fetched a rod of quince-tree and continued beating me on the back and sides till I lost consciousness. Then he commanded the slaves to take me away as soon as it was dark to the house wherein I dwelt before my marriage. They did their lord's bidding and cast me down in my old home and went their ways. I lay confined to my bed for four months before I was able to rise and health returned to me. ⬩⬩⬩ At the end of that time I went to the house where all this had happened and found it a ruin; the street had been pulled down endlong and rubbish-heaps rose where the building erst was; nor could I learn how this had come about. Then I betook myself to this my sister on my father's side and found her with these two black bitches. I told her the whole of my story and then she told me her own story, and we abode together and the subject of marriage was never on our tongues for all these years. After a while we were joined by our other sister, the procuratrix, who goeth out every morning and buyeth all we require for the day and night; and we continued in such condition till this last night. ⬩⬩⬩ In the morning our sister went out, as usual, and then befel us what befel from bringing the Porter into the house and admitting these three Kalandar-men. We entreated them kindly and honourably, and a quarter of the night had not passed ere three respectable merchants from Mosul joined us and told us their adventures. We sat talking with them but on one condition, which they violated; whereupon we treated them as sorted with their breach of promise, and made them repeat the account they had given of themselves. They did our bidding and we forgave their offence; so they departed from us and this morning we were unexpectedly summoned to thy presence. And such is our story! ～～ The Caliph wondered at her words and — — And Shahrazad perceived the dawn of day and ceased saying her say.

*When it was the Thirteenth Night*

Shahrazad continued. It hath reached me, O auspicious King, that the Caliph commanded this story and those of the sister and the Kalandars to be recorded in the archives. Then he asked the eldest lady, "Knowest thou the whereabouts of the Ifritah who spelled thy sisters?" and she answered, "O Commander of the Faithful, she gave me a ringlet of her hair saying: 'Whenas thou wouldest see me, burn these hairs and I will be with thee forthright.'" ～～ Quoth the Caliph, "Bring me hither the hair." ～～ She brought it and he threw the whole lock upon the fire. As soon as the odour of the burning hair dispread itself, the palace trembled, and all present heard a rolling of thunder and a noise as of wings and lo! the Jinniyah stood in the Caliph's presence. She saluted him and said, "Know that this damsel delivered me from death and destroyed mine enemy. Now I had seen how her sisters dealt with her and felt myself bound to avenge her on them. At first I was minded to slay them, but I feared it would be grievous to her, so I transformed them to bitches; but if thou desire their release, O Commander of the Faithful, I will release them to pleasure thee." ～～ Quoth the Caliph, "Release them and after we will look into the affair of the beaten lady; and if the truth of her story be evidenced I will exact retaliation from him who wronged her." ～～ Said the Ifritah, "O Commander of the Faithful, the man who did that deed by this lady is the nearest of all men to thee!" ～～ So saying she took a cup of water and uttered words there was no

understanding; then she sprinkled some of the water over the faces of the two bitches, saying, "Return to your former human shape!" whereupon they were restored. Then said the Ifritah, "O Commander of the Faithful, of a truth he who scourged this lady with rods is thy son; for he had heard of her beauty and loveliness and married her according to the law and committed the crime (such as it is) of scourging her. Yet indeed he is not to be blamed for beating her, for he laid a condition on her and swore her by a solemn oath not to do a certain thing; however, she was false to her vow." When the Caliph heard these words and knew who had beaten the damsel, he marvelled with mighty marvel and said, "And now by Allah, we will do a deed which shall be recorded of us after we are no more." Then he summoned his son and questioned him of the story of the portress; and he told it in the face of truth; whereupon the Caliph bade call into presence the Kazis and their witnesses and the three Kalandars and the first lady with her sisters-german who had been ensorcelled. And he married the three to the three Kalandars and he appointed them chamberlains about his person, assigning to them stipends and all that they required, and lodging them in his palace at Baghdad. He returned the beaten lady to his son, renewing the marriage-contract between them. As for himself he took to wife the procuratrix. And the people marvelled at their Caliph's generosity and natural beneficence and princely wisdom. And this, O auspicious King, is the end of their story.

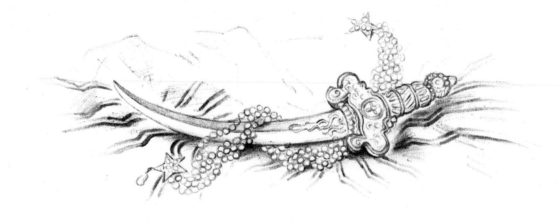

And in this wise Shahrazad continued. Each night, for a thousand nights and a night, Dunyazad asked of her sister to recite some new story, delightsome and delectable; and Shahrazad would begin, "It is related, O auspicious King." ⟶ And so, when Shahrazad had ended her final tale, she arose to her feet and, kissing the ground before him, said, "O King of the time and unique one, for a thousand nights and a night I have entertained thee with stories of folk gone before. May I then make bold to crave a boon of thee? Release me from the doom of death that I may rear thy children as they should be reared!" ⟶ When the king heard this, he wept and said, "By Allah, O Shahrazad, I pardoned thee long before the coming of thy children, for that I found thee pure and chaste and ingenuous and pious. I take the Almighty to witness me that I exempt thee from aught that can harm thee." And Shahrazad kissed his feet and rejoiced. ⟶ In due time, King Shahryar summoned the chroniclers and copyists and bade them write all that had betided him with his wife, and so they wrote it, and the tales were copied again and dispread throughout the land. And the people named them *The Marvels of the Thousand Nights and a Night.* ⟶ This is all that hath come down to us of the origins of the book, and Allah is All-knowing.

ACKNOWLEDGMENTS

I could not have created this book without the invaluable contributions of many people: those who loaned garments and props, made costumes and jewelry, helped with fittings and make-up, the numerous models, the photographers, and those who offered assistance and consultation throughout. I am grateful to all of the following: Angel Adorno, Suzanne Aichinger, Alvaro, Bloomingdale's, Ray Brown, Conroy Campbell, Carlos, Arturo Castillo, Angelo Colon, Fernando Colon, Maria Luisa Cruz, Gary De Sclafani, Doze, Bill Erb, Fable, Ruth Ann Fredenthal, Kathleen Gates, Natalia Gervais, Rebecca Ghiglieri, Alex Gotfryd, Mike Hare, Brenda Hoffman, Robert Isebel, Iza Kosova, Francine Landes, Kenneth Jay Lane, Fred Lansac, Darral Lewis, Claudja McDonnell, Ari Marchand, Feliciano Martinez, Max, Casie Milét, Claudio Motta, Bill Niemeier, Matthew Olszak, Garon Peterson, Paul Quadley, Tyrone Randall, Renaldo, Evelyn Santos, Clifford Skelton, Stella, Scott Sterling, Jane Thorvaldson, Tom Trabbic, Vangelis, Laurence Vetu, David Vignon, Eugenie Vincent, Vivian, Eric Walters, Jason Watson, Lara Wheeler, Blair Wilfley, David Wolfson, Gracie Wolfson, Zeta. Special thanks to Jean-Eudes Canival.

Design

*J. C. Suarès*
*Laurence Vetu*

Production

*Katherine van Kessel*
*Carol Chien*

*Composed in Cochin by U.S. Lithograph Inc.,*
*New York, New York*
*Printed and bound by Dai Nippon Printing Co., Ltd.,*
*Tokyo, Japan*